THE LADY SAID NO

An Augustus Grant Mystery

JACQUIE BIGGAR

Wavefront Publishing

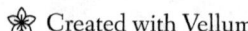

For those in the Thoroughbred racing industry fighting to correct the ill treatment of these beautiful animals.

Where there is mystery, it is generally suspected there must also be evil.

— LORD BYRON

What Readers Are Saying

The Guardian

Who wouldn't want to be swept off her feet by a movie star? And championed by a guardian angel? Sign me up! And like any great start to a series, the ending left me reaching for the next book. Highly recommended
     Christine Hart

I was lucky to receive an advanced copy of The Guardian. A quick, easy read that I enjoyed!. A serious topic handled not only with touching moments but a few humorous moments also. Romance, suspense, family ties, friendship, angels that aren't sure about being angels, some sad moments, some nail biter moments, and a darling dog named Sugar Bear....what more could we want? I'm looking forward to the next book in this series.

Barbara Cassata

The Sheriff Meets His Match

Who could possibly be the perfect match for Sheriff Jack Garrett, the steadfast pillar of a small west coast town like Tidal Falls? Enter Laurel Thomas, a woman on the run from her past in Florida. As soon as she shows up in Tidal Falls, she turns Jack's meticulously organized world upside down with her disorganized ways, sexy looks and feisty humor. I'd been craving Jack's story every since I read about him in an earlier story in the Wounded Hearts series, and I wasn't disappointed! Ms Biggar's characters leap off the page and become family you'll be rooting for with all your heart.

Jacqui Nelson

I really enjoyed this romance. It has a heroine that's running around helping family, while working for the sheriff. She uses sticky notes to help keep everything straight, while the family tends to count on her to make everything right. This is full of humor and a little bit of serious in a small town type setting. I've given it a rating of 4.5*. It really made me laugh.

Nancy Luebke

Twilight's Encore

What a captivating story. Twilight's Encore is the third book

of Wounded Hearts series. This is Ty's and Katy's story, i have

to say what a beautiful story!!!

Nicole- Reading Alley

This is a very heartwarming, suspenseful book that will have you cheering for the good guys. HIGHLY RECOMMEND and Can't wait for Book 4 in the Wounded Hearts series.

Barbara

The Rebel's Redemption

What I loved about this story was not only the premise but how it all came together.

LAS reviewer

THE REBEL'S REDEMPTION (*Wounded Hearts,* #2) *by Jacquie Biggar had me reading this romantic suspense well past my bedtime. The characters are so well written they could walk right off the page!*

Avonna-The Romance Reviews

The Lady Said No

CHANDLER  COUNTY

Preface

The Race is on to find a Killer in the heart of Kentucky horse country

Detective Augustus Grant is faced with his most baffling case to date. Well-respected race horse breeder, John Jorgenson, is murdered in his den days before the Kentucky Derby and the list of suspects is growing.

Complicating matters, Gus' ex-girlfriend is the last person to have seen the victim alive.

Rebecca Hayes owes the Jorgenson family her loyalty. They gave her a new life after a disastrous affair leaves her alone and pregnant.

With all the evidence pointing in Becky's direction, will Gus do his duty?

Or follow his heart?

Excerpt

That was interesting. He'd heard rumors around town the Jorgensons were in financial straits, but he'd put it down to jealousy and human nature. Obviously, there was more to the story than he'd figured.

Maybe even enough for murder?

Gus finished the soup and thanked the young cook before making his way into the main part of the house. Fine hardwood floors and the dark wainscoting lined the walls. Everything was polished to within an inch of its life and glistened from top to bottom. How could anyone feel comfortable in a place like this? Bet the Jorgensons never kicked their feet up to relax, or left their rooms in robes in search of a midnight snack. This was the type of house that demanded decorum.

As if to prove his verdict, a man came into view at the end of the hall. He was directing the coroner,

Nancy Huggins, to a room with a police guard, disapproval radiating from his immaculate frame. He wore a suit nicer than Gus' funeral attire, all three pieces starched and pressed to perfection. A wrinkle wouldn't dare latch itself to those clothes.

Gus looked down at his own rumpled shirt and skewed tie and shrugged.

Nancy caught his eye and raised her brow. "Augustus. What brings you to the back of beyond?"

The manservant turned, and a chill crawled down Gus' back. The guy had the deadest, black eyes he'd ever seen.

"I'm...ah, here to investigate the Jorgenson case. The Brass called and requested me for this one."

"Hmm, must be important then. I heard you received a medal from the President."

He squirmed.

He hadn't done anything to deserve a medal. It was pure luck that he figured out the plot to kidnap the President's daughter, and was able to catch the perps before they got away with the deed.

"Why were you in the back of the house, *sir?* That area is reserved for the servants." The manservant folded his arms and waited for an answer. Gus felt like a misbehaving child all over again.

"I, ah... came in from the pool, after talking to Mrs. Jorgenson. She gave me permission to question the staff as I see fit." He met the man's coal dark gaze. "And you are?"

Gus didn't think it was possible for the broom handle to climb any further up the man's butt.

"That's Ernest. He takes a while to warm up to strangers," a lilting voice drifted down from the upper reaches of the home.

Gus froze. His heart battered the walls of his chest. There was a ringing in his ears. The chicken soup threatened to revolt.

"Hello, Augustus."

Chapter One

pril 16, 1953

A Augustus Grant drove slowly down the gravel drive lined with towering oaks waving gently in the early spring breeze. A split rail fence kept him company, the boards gleaming with a fresh coat of whitewash. In the distance, he could see some fine-looking horses munching on the blue-green grass Kentucky was famous for, not that he was any judge of horseflesh. A couple of foals, their chestnut coats gleaming in the early morning sun, broke away from the herd, kicking and jumping like skittish deer.

He stopped and rolled down his window, sticking his nose in the air to catch a whiff of how the other half lived. Money. He smelled money. If there one thing the aristocracy knew, it was how to live in style.

Case in point; the mansion had just come into

view. A Georgian red brick structure, three stories tall, with four thick white columns supporting the upper balcony, and enough windows to keep a cleaner busy for a year. It was truly awe-inspiring. Much different from his little two-room bungalow in town, that's for sure.

Gus pulled up behind the sheriff's car and nodded to the officer guarding the front door. Sheriff Tromley wasn't going to be happy to see him. He tended to be territorial over his cases, but the chief had insisted, so here he was.

He took his time, gathering the leather briefcase that had been a gift from his ex-wife, his keys, a spare pen, and his trench coat in case the weather turned, rolled up the window and opened the door. Except now his hands were full and he couldn't get out of the car. It took a few moments and some cringing when he inadvertently hit the horn with his elbow, but Gus finally managed to exit the Buick.

"Need any help, sir?" The young officer glanced doubtfully at the steep staircase leading up to the double entrance doors, then at him as though he were an old man in need of a walker.

Gus straightened his tie, darn near giving himself a shiner with the corner of the briefcase, and shook his head. "I can manage, thank you. Mind telling me where the sheriff is?"

"Out back, sir. Talking to the widow."

That made sense. It was an established fact that in eighty-eight percent of murder cases, the killer was someone who knew the victim. He waited until the officer pointed which direction he should go, then Gus trudged down the walk, reviewing the circumstances in his head.

Dead male, approximately fifty-five years of age, found on the floor in his den with a gunshot wound to the head. The Jorgenson family were fourth generation horse breeders, and even had a colt who had won two of three legs in the Triple Crown. Gus had heard the horse was making the Jorgenson family more money now as a stud than he had racing. Nice way to retire.

He rounded the corner of the house, avoided the giant rose bush reaching out to grab his clothes, and sought out the elusive sheriff. There he was, on the other side of an Olympic-sized swimming pool, complete with waterfall. A gazebo provided both shelter and privacy from the house, but Gus could see just fine. And what he saw pulled him up short.

The sheriff had his arms wrapped around a woman who barely cleared his chest, her raven locks spilling down the back of her crimson red robe as she tilted her head to gaze into his eyes.

Augustus cleared his throat and the woman jumped, freeing herself from the sheriff's embrace.

Tromley glared across the distance, hands fisted at his sides, while the woman, Gus was sure it was the widow Jorgenson from the description he'd been given, spun away, tightening the belt on her bathrobe. As he neared, she picked up a pack of cigarettes with trembling fingers and lit a smoke. She took a long drag and exhaled, a blue cloud forming a nimbus around her head.

"What are you doing here, Detective?" The sheriff crossed his arms over a barrel chest and scowled.

"Well, sir," Gus started, then tripped over a step and almost went sprawling. "The, ah, chief asked me to come out and offer a hand. He's worried what the press is going to do with this one. Mr. Jorgenson is..." The woman let out a soft cry. "I mean *was*, sorry Ma'am." He cleared his throat. "Mr. Jorgenson *was* a prominent member of the Lexington community."

"We're aware of John's standing in the community, Detective Grant," the sheriff said impatiently. "There's no need for you to be here. I just finished my interview with Mrs. Jorgenson and will have a report filed by this afternoon. It was clearly suicide. These things happen." He glanced at the widow and his expression softened. "Trudy has been through enough. She's the one who found her husband in the den." His gaze hardened as it returned to Gus. "I'm sure you'll understand if she needs some space right now to gather herself."

4

Gus hesitated, then nodded to the missus. "Sorry for your loss, ma'am. Take all the time you need. Mind if I step inside, maybe have a look at the crime scene? Question your staff?" He ignored the sheriff's soft curse. "It's just that it's the chief's orders and all. I won't be long..." He waited while she made eye contact with the sheriff, and when she began to shake her head, he added, "Or I could start with you, ma'am, if you would prefer?"

"Grant," the sheriff warned.

Mrs. Jorgenson sighed and stubbed out her cigarette on an elegant cut-crystal ashtray in the center of the table. "It seems you're determined, Detective. Go ahead then, question my staff. But don't get in their way. They have jobs to do, same as you."

She sank into a deeply piled armchair and crossed slender legs, making no effort to stop the robe from sliding open dangerously high on her thigh. And of course she caught him looking. A feline smile temporarily chased the shadows from her eyes. "Anything else, Detective?"

A cold shower maybe?

Gus cleared his throat and fumbled with his briefcase. "Uh, no, thank you, ma'am. Appreciated."

He turned and stumbled down the same dang step he'd tripped on earlier. He couldn't imagine any man voluntarily giving her up, but you never knew what happened behind closed doors. He'd have a quick look-see, talk to a couple staff members, and be on his way. Case closed.

Except—it kind of bothered him. Shouldn't she be a little more heartbroken at the loss of her husband? Shock triggered different reactions depending on the person, of course, but she'd seemed more worried about the staff getting their jobs done than getting to the truth. And what was going on between her and the sheriff?

He glanced surreptitiously over his shoulder and caught what seemed to be a heated exchange between the widow and the lawman. Obviously, they weren't strangers. In fact, if he wasn't mistaken, he'd have to say they had a history. Question was; how recent?

Chapter Two

CHANDLER  COUNTY

Rebecca Hayes stood at the window, her arms laden with freshly ironed linens, and stared down at the drama unfolding below. There was another man out there now besides the sheriff. Mrs. J looked upset. She always chain-smoked when she was stressed. Which was often.

The police had arrived about an hour ago. Rebecca heard the sirens and had raced upstairs, anxious to check on her daughter. To cuddle her happy, healthy little body and try not to think about her boss lying dead on the floor of the den.

The man turned to come back to the house and stumbled on the steps around the swimming pool. Rebecca would have smiled if she didn't notice the daggers her mistress was throwing at his back.

Who was this man?

Something about his dark head and broad shoulders told her he was going to bring a whole ton of trouble to the Jorgenson household. As though there wasn't enough of that to go around already.

She'd awoken this morning to her mistress's shrieks for help. By the time she'd dressed and hurried two flights down to the main floor, pandemonium had broken out. Her friend, Jocelyn, had grabbed her hand and pulled her aside as some of the ranch hands filled the entrance to the den, their faces grim.

"You don't want to go in there, Becky, it's bad," Jocelyn had whispered, eyes filled with horrified tears.

"What's going on? Where's the witch?" As their boss's wife was often called—behind her back, of course.

"Mrs. J found him," Jocelyn said, her voice quivering. "He musta shot himself in the head. There ain't nothing left." She'd lifted a shaking hand to her mouth and ran for the nearby bathroom, dodging the disapproving gaze of Mr. Jorgenson's manservant, Ernest.

Rebecca's heart had pounded, the blood rushing from her head. She'd grabbed the newel post on the staircase and sank to the bottom step. How could this have happened? Mr. Jorgenson was well-respected. He had so much; the perfect house, the trophy wife, a successful career. Why would he do this? It didn't make sense.

He'd called her to the den a few nights ago. When she had arrived, it was to find him slumped in a tufted leather armchair in front of a roaring fire, even though it had been unseasonably warm for the past week. He'd been holding his favourite bronze statue in his lap and a glass of amber liquid, the snifter on the side table at his elbow almost empty.

He'd barely glanced up when she knocked and entered through the partially open door. "Come in, my dear. Have a seat."

Rebecca hesitated, her nose wrinkling at the stench of alcohol. "What is it, sir? Can't it wait 'til morning? It's rather late."

He ignored her and stared into the flames. "You ever wish you could change the past, Miss Hayes?"

A couple of years ago she would have answered with an unequivocal yes, but that was before she held her baby girl in her arms for the first time and gazed upon the Lord's most priceless gift—life.

"No, sir." She eased into the chair across from him and soaked up the warmth from the fire. It had been chilly in the sewing room at the back of the house where she'd spent the last few hours re-hemming Mrs. Jorgenson's dress for the big dinner party coming up in a couple of weeks. The expensive satin of the empire-waisted gown was unforgiving of any bodily imperfections. Not that Mrs. J had any; she hardly ever ate and regularly swam in the pool behind the house.

"I do." Mr. Jorgenson's melancholy voice startled her. She gazed at him slouched in the too-big chair cradling that sculpture, and sympathy tightened her chest. He knew of his second wife's infidelity; she could see it in the miserable expression and the now emptied glass dangling from his hand like a lost love.

"Sir..." she hesitated, not sure what could be said to ease his pain. "It's late, Mr. Jorgenson. Maybe things will look better in the morning. You should get some rest. The big day is coming." His favored colt, Forever Humble, was slated to run in the Kentucky Derby the beginning of May. The entire ranch had been undergoing a renovation in preparation for the after-party. They were all in need of a break, but it wouldn't happen until everything was perfect, hence the refitting of Mrs. J's gown.

Rebecca stifled a sudden yawn and glanced at the cuckoo clock hanging behind the desk. Almost midnight. Too late to be sitting alone in a dark den with her boss. Her gaze landed once more on the Remington sculpture of an Aboriginal warrior holding the skull of a bull above his head. Icy fingers crept up her spine.

She jerked her gaze back to her host, relieved to see he had apparently dozed off. She carefully rose, cringing at the creak of leather upholstery giving up its burden. Careful not to disturb Mr. Jorgenson, she eased the statue from his lax grip and replaced it on his desk. A few steps later and she was almost home free.

"Live your dreams, Miss Hayes," he muttered, half-awake, half-alcohol induced languor. "Life's too short. You need to live your dreams."

Hand on the door knob, Rebecca hesitated, loathe to leave him there. He seemed so very alone. She wasn't even sure why he'd asked for her in the first place. They'd rarely had anything to do with each other since she'd taken the job two years ago. It wasn't easy for a single mother to find work and she'd been elated to hear the Jorgensons were looking for a live-in seamstress. It wasn't the career she'd wished for, but she didn't have much choice. And luckily, it had worked out—for the most part anyway.

"I plan to, sir. Good night, Mr. Jorgenson."

And that was the last time she would ever see him.

Chapter Three

CHANDLER COUNTY

Gus entered the back vestibule and halted for a moment, soaking up the silence. His grannie always told him these old houses would speak if he just listened. He believed her too. There was something about plantation homes that seemed to conjure up ghosts from the past. Many were built before the civil war era and filled with the grandest furniture, their walls steeped in history.

Someone humming a mournful tune from the next room drew him to a large, open-plan kitchen, refitted with all the latest appliances. A young black woman stood at the gas stove stirring something that smelled enticingly like chicken soup, going by the intoxicating scent. Her hair was tucked into a tight bun and held in place by a bright red head scarf.

Gus cleared his throat and the lady let out a little

shriek. A quick grab saved the utensil from the boiling pot, but he could see she'd burned her hand by the way she cupped it close to her body.

"What you doing comin' in the back door and scaring the bejesus out of me like that?" She brandished the spoon like she was ready to tan his hide and hang it out to dry.

"Sorry, miss. You should get that hand under some cool water. Burns like that, they tend to get infected. I've seen it. You don't want that, ma'am." He held up his badge. "I'm Detective Grant. I was ah... wondering if ya'll had a moment to answer a few questions on the death of Mr. Jorgenson."

Her pretty face fell, her eyes turning into dark pools of sadness. She set the spoon down to run some water for her hand. When she turned back, it was swathed with a snowy white towel and she had her expression wrapped up just as tight. "What is it, you wants to know?"

She pulled out a straight back chair from the wooden kitchen table, and sat, her skirts flouncing out around her body like flower petals.

Gus rubbed his chin and ambled over to the pot of soup, drawn by the aroma onion and herbs. His stomach growled. He grimaced, well aware it had been twelve hours or more since his last meal.

"This sure does smell fine, Miss...?"

"Rose," she slowly answered. "Jocelyn Rose. Chicken soup is Ms. Jorgenson's favorite. I thought today..." She sniffled and held the bandaged hand to her mouth.

"Ah... yes, miss. That's real nice of you." He looked into the pot and practically salivated. "Mind if I try a bit, Miss Jocelyn?"

Her eyes narrowed. She lowered the cloth and sighed, starting to rise. "I guess it would be alright."

Gus waved her down. "No, stay there. I can do it." He searched out a bowl and spoon, spied a hunk of homemade bread, cut a thick slice, and brought everything to the table. He set the bowl down and sloshed onto the pristine white tablecloth. She tut-tutted and began to clamber to her feet, but Gus waved her down and hurried to the sink for a washcloth.

"Sorry about that. I'm not usually so clumsy." *Ha.* His nose was going to grow for sure.

By the time he got the mess cleaned up, his jacket stowed away, and his cuffs turned back, she was looking more than a little disconcerted. Perfect.

So was the soup. He almost moaned with the first taste, it was that good. "No wonder Mrs. Jorgenson likes this so much. You're a whiz." He took another couple of bites, then dipped the bread in the bowl. He started to lift it to his mouth, then eyed the cook over the top. "Any idea who would do this horrible thing, miss?"

She been sitting there, smiling over his enjoyment of the meal. The words seemed to catch her by surprise and her eyes widened. He was curious about the shadow that darkened her expression.

"If there's something you want to share; it would be just between the two of us." He waved the bread in the air.

She hesitated, then glanced around before leaning close. "Mr. Jorgenson was real worried about his horse, Forever Humble. I thinks he has a lot invested in the race. Emmett says he's been hanging out at the track night and day." She covered her face with her hands, one bandaged white, one black. "It's just so sad."

Hmm. That was interesting. He'd heard rumors around town the Jorgensons were in financial straits, but he'd put it down to jealousy and human nature. Obviously, there was more to the story than he'd figured.

Maybe even enough for murder?

Gus finished the soup and thanked the young cook before making his way into the main part of the house. Fine hardwood floors and the dark wainscoting lined the walls. Everything was polished to within an inch of its life and glistened from top to bottom. How could anyone feel comfortable in a place like this? Bet the

Jorgensons never kicked their feet up to relax, or left their rooms in robes in search of a midnight snack. This was the type of house that demanded decorum.

As if to prove his verdict, a man came into view at the end of the hall. He was directing the coroner, Nancy Huggins, to a room with a police guard, disapproval radiating from his immaculate frame. He wore a suit nicer than Gus' funeral attire, all three pieces starched and pressed to perfection. A wrinkle wouldn't dare latch itself to those clothes.

Gus looked down at his own rumpled shirt and skewed tie and shrugged.

Nancy caught his eye and raised her brow. "Augustus. What brings you to the back of beyond?"

The manservant turned, and a chill crawled down Gus' back. The guy had the deadest, black eyes he'd ever seen.

"I'm...ah, here to investigate the Jorgenson case. The Brass called and requested me for this one."

"Hmm, must be important then. I heard you received a medal from the President."

Gus squirmed.

He hadn't done anything to deserve a medal. It was pure luck he'd figured out the plot to kidnap the President's daughter, and was able to catch the perps before they got away with the deed.

"Why were you in the back of the house, *sir?* That

area is reserved for the servants." The manservant folded his arms and waited for an answer. Gus felt like a misbehaving child all over again.

"I, ah... came in from the pool, after talking to Mrs. Jorgenson. She gave me permission to question the staff as I see fit." He met the man's coal dark gaze. "And you are?"

Gus didn't think it was possible for the broom handle to climb any further up the man's butt.

"That's Ernest. He takes a while to warm up to strangers," a lilting voice drifted down from the upper reaches of the home.

Gus froze. His heart battered the walls of his chest. There was a ringing in his ears. The chicken soup threatened to revolt.

"Hello, Augustus."

Chapter Four

Forever Humble whickered a greeting, leaning his shapely head over the door of his stall as Steve entered the stables. That horse had the sweetest temperament of any thoroughbred he'd ever had the pleasure to work with. A gorgeous bay, sixteen hands tall, with bloodlines tracing back to the famous Darley Arabian and sired by Polynesian, he'd proven himself on the track, winning all but one of his races so far. But, the ultimate test was yet to come.

And Steve had misgivings.

He rubbed Humble's velvety soft muzzle and offered him his favorite treat, a juicy carrot, but the horse turned his head away. Steve frowned and opened the stall door, running practiced hands down the animal's sloped chest and fetlocks. No hint of heat or swelling that he could find. Still, maybe a visit from the vet was called for. He'd have to run it by Jorgenson first though. It never made sense to him why the boss didn't mind paying a fortune for flowers and booze to celebrate the Derby, but penny-pinched when it came to his stables. If it weren't for Humble here, he'd have moved on by now. There was no shortage of work for a trainer who produced Kentucky Derby winners, and Steve did. He knew his animals; hell, he practically lived with them during training season. To him horses were far more reliable than humans.

Especially the female variety.

He stopped to check Humble's water, making sure the stable hand had filled it fresh as he'd been ordered, and that the colt's stall was clean, before exiting the cubicle and working toward his office. He had several stops along the way. Horses were curious by nature, and many had come to the door of their enclosures to watch him walk by. This was his world; he didn't know any other way. Steve's taciturn father, Roger McMillon, a famous trainer in his time, had taught his son the secret of his professional success—listen to the animal. It had helped him immeasurably as a jockey.

It was so simple, and yet many in the industry ignored it in the rush to become the best. Horses were like athletes, they needed hours upon hours of training, but they also needed companionship, rest, and care. Unlike many trainers, Steve didn't believe in pushing his animals more than necessary. They gave their best because they trusted him, it was that easy.

His desk was piled with papers he never seemed to have time to go through, stats, auction listings, race forms, workout calendars. He needed a damn secretary. He sat on the wooden straight-back chair and reached for the phone to dial the main house. His gaze roamed while he waited. Various pedigree charts lined the walls, competing for space with shelves of liniment, gauze, bridles, bits and polish, all the tools of the trade. Over in the corner a barrel with his special blend of grain lay under lock and key. He didn't trust anyone with the recipe. It had been passed to him by his father, and it worked. Used sparingly, it gave his horses a fighting chance at the winner's cup.

"Yes?" The Jorgenson's manservant came on the line.

"I need to speak to Mr. Jorgenson," he growled. There was something about Ernest that always got his hackles up.

"What do you want, McMillon?" The snooty English accent carried more than a hint of disdain.

Steve swore under his breath. He didn't have time for this crap. "Is he there, or isn't he?"

"I'm not at liberty to say," the manservant answered.

This was ridiculous. Two weeks away from the race of a lifetime and he was getting the runaround.

"What about Tru... Mrs. Jorgenson then?" he said impatiently.

"I believe she has... company," the smart-ass replied.

Fine, he'd call the vet and worry about repercussions later.

"Thanks." *For nothing*. Steve hung up and placed the call to Doc Baker in Bourbonville. The doctor was in surgery, but his receptionist assured him he'd be out to the ranch before the end of the day. He replaced the phone on the hook, but couldn't get Ernest's cryptic words off his mind. What did he mean by *company*?

He'd known going into it an affair with the boss's wife was career suicide, but he hadn't been able to control his lust. And she'd played him like a freaking violin. At least he'd had the sense to end the relationship before any lasting damage was done, other than stomping his heart into the Kentucky dirt beneath her shoe. The dame knew how to pack a punch, there was no denying that. He still couldn't believe she'd threatened him. As if he would ever tell. If she lived up to her words, she would destroy not only his career, but his father's good name also.

He looked at the barrel of feed again and his stomach rolled.

BECKY STOOD AT THE TOP OF THE GRAND STAIRCASE and felt the world give way.

Augustus.

It had been too long.

And not long enough.

She couldn't believe he was here. Or maybe she could. It had always been his dream to become a detective. After all, that was the reason they had split up, wasn't it? He'd craved the excitement, and she'd needed stability. Safety.

Well, it was too late now, on many levels. The best thing she could do would be to put on a brave face and escape with her pride.

"Hello, Augustus," she called. Careful not to let him see her trembling, she gripped the banister and reluctantly went to join the man who had stolen her heart. He was every bit as tall as she remembered. Still just as handsome, too. A few more lines around the eyes and mouth maybe. She shied away from his lips, focusing instead on the crooked tie and wrinkled shirt. A wry smile touched her mouth.

"I see you still haven't figured out the right side of an iron," she murmured.

He glanced down and ran a strong, tanned hand down his chest. Something fluttered to life in hers.

He met her gaze with a grin that slowly faded away. "I looked for you," he said.

Oh, God.

This wasn't what she expected. After leaving Bourbonville and moving here, to Balmoral, she'd second-guessed her decision often, but never realized maybe he did too, just a little.

"You're the cop. You could have found me if you tried."

"You know this... gentleman?" Ernest asked, reminding her they had an audience.

She glared, warning Augustus to keep quiet, before meeting the butler's gaze head-on. "Mr. Grant and I went to the same school. We... fell out of touch," she stammered.

"Hmm," was all the manservant said. "Well, if you'll follow me, Mr. Grant, I'll direct you to the den where the master..." He stopped and turned away, heading toward the double doors, closed for privacy. Mr. Jorgenson preferred it that way.

Not that he'd know the difference now.

Rebecca choked back a sob. Gus moved as though to hug her before realizing his work friends were watching. He gave her a helpless look and followed Ernest to the door.

Rebecca watched until he disappeared from view, her heart shattering into a thousand pieces she didn't know if she could put back together again.

Chapter Five

Gus followed the stiff-necked manservant to the door of the den, though his emotions were tugging him back to Rebecca like a starved man to a banquet.

He couldn't believe how beautiful she'd become. She'd always been pretty, but now there was an added maturity to her features that suited her face. The tomboy figure he fondly remembered had become hills and valleys he ached to explore. They'd been best friends, then lovers, then enemies. It'd been his fault, that was the worst of it. He'd let his drive for a career ruin the only good thing in his life. He could tell himself he'd done his part. After getting his degree and returning to Bourbonville he had tried to find her. But she was right, he hadn't tried hard enough.

Their relationship had already been floundering; it

had seemed easier to let it die a natural death. He regretted that now. One glimpse of her had brought back all the old feelings. Memories of happier times.

Ernest reached for the door knob and was stopped by the officer on guard.

"Sorry, only trained personnel are allowed."

Ernest glared at him. "I've worked in this household for

years; I believe I *am* trained."

The sergeant exchanged a helpless glance with Gus. "I'm sorry, sir. Those are the rules."

Gus stepped between the two men before a full-scale war broke out. "It's okay, sergeant." He flipped open his badge. "I'm Detective Grant. The..." He waved a hand toward the butler.

Ernest lowered his brows. "Manservant."

Gus nodded. "*Manservant*, was just showing me the way to the crime scene."

The officer checked his badge, then reached back to open the door. The stench of death was immediate, a toxic mix of human waste impossible to forget. Gus turned his head to draw one last clean breath and met Rebecca's anxious gaze.

That look gave him pause.

Why was she worried? Just how well did Rebecca know the owner of Balmoral?

"Coming, Detective?" The sergeant's voice interrupted his musings. Gus shrugged off his misgivings and followed the man into the room, sliding past the grim-faced Ernest.

Nancy knelt by the victim, her hands covered with white gloves and booties on her feet. She glanced up when he walked in and pointed at his shoes. Gus dug through his coat pockets until he found his booties, put them on, nodded to the sergeant, and made his way over to her side.

"It's a bad one," she said, turning attention to her preliminary findings. "Single shot to the temple, through and through. Near as I can tell, time of death was sometime between midnight and three a.m., no sign of defensive wounds." She stopped and gazed at him with world-weary eyes. "Who would do this, Augustus?"

Gus observed the brain matter splattered on the leather tufted chair and rich, red Aubusson carpet and his stomach churned. His first thought was *crime of passion*. There had been some effort made to set the scene up as a suicide. The gun rested in the victim's open hand, finger wrapped around the trigger. A cut crystal tumbler lay on its side nearby, a stain wetting the carpet. Gus touched the wet spot and sniffed, rubbing the tips of his fingers—bourbon. The good kind. Not something a man bent on ending his own life would let go to waste.

"I'm not sure, Nancy, but I do know the brass will be all over this one, so take your time, okay? We don't want to miss anything."

She huffed out an indignant breath. "You telling me how to do my job, now?"

He held up a hand to halt her blistering tongue. "The Jorgensons are big news, that's all I'm saying. Don't they have a horse in the Derby this year?"

The sergeant, who had remained by the door, and watched their exchange with interest, piped up. "Forever Humble. Lots of money riding on that colt." His face became animated. "You ever see him race, Detective? He's some kind of fast. Likes to run the outside track. Gives me a heart attack every time."

Gus smiled. "You a betting man...?"

"Fish, sir. Everyone calls me Fish."

Nancy chuckled and the young man's neck turned brick red.

"I'm not a gambler, no sir, but I admit I like to spend a Saturday now and then down at the track. It's some exciting. You ever been, Mr. Grant?"

Gus shook his head. "No, can't say as I have. Not that fond of horses, though I guess that's the wrong thing to say in this house." He admired the landscape watercolor on the wall, rolling hills with a herd of wild horses barreling straight at him, eyes crazy and manes flying as though they were about to burst the confines of paint and canvas.

"Augustus, there's something you need to see." Nancy's voice was muffled as she stretched, shapely butt in the air, to reach something under the leather chair. She grunted and tugged until a bronze sculpture came into view. When she stood it on the carpet, he saw it was about twelve inches in height, a warrior on a horse, raised arm carrying a spear.

"There's blood and hair fragments," she said, turning it carefully to inspect the evidence. "I can't be sure until I get it to the lab, but this looks like a match to our vic."

Well, that explained why there were no defensive wounds. The poor sop probably didn't know what hit him. Gus looked around until he found the suspiciously empty spot on the desk. He gave a wide berth to the corpse, conscious of Nancy's critical gaze. The desk was one of those massive claw-foot affairs, mahogany maybe, rich and elegant instead of simply functional. He pulled a linen handkerchief out of his pocket and checked the drawers. An assortment of papers greeted him, some on household expenses, most on Jorgenson's passion—thoroughbreds. Nothing that looked like a cause for murder.

Gus was about to replace the documents when a slip of yellowed paper lodged in the back of the drawer caught his eye. He reached in, using the hankie, and retrieved the handwritten note.

Do what I told you to do, or the truth will destroy you

The threat inherent on the scrap of paper chilled his blood. There was trouble brewing in the Jorgenson household, and Gus was afraid Rebecca was somehow involved.

Chapter Six

Gus wandered the length of the massive Jorgenson stables in awe. The exterior was grand enough; three giant cupolas and the clapboard siding painted eye-blinding white with black trim—the team's winning colors—but then he entered the interior and was amazed by the sheer size of the building. Wrought iron lamps hung beside each stall, all shining light on the gold-etched labels with the occupant's name. Dancing Queen, Harley's Revenge, Annabelle Lady; fancy names for expensive animals.

He wrinkled his nose, picking up the scents of hay, leather, horse, and an underlying aroma of manure. Men hurried from stall to stall, buckets and shovels in hand, glancing curiously at him as they passed. A couple of the horses leaned over and eyed him with disdain glittering out of chocolate brown eyes. And with good reason, these critters had it made. They were treated like royalty; bathed, picked up after, fed the very best food money could buy, exercised, groomed, photographed, some even had statues made in their honor. When Gus came back in his next life, he wanted to be a Thoroughbred.

He rubbed his itchy eyes. Scratch that. His hay fever would drive him crazy if he was a horse.

"Can I help you?" A man filled the doorway to the office, his scowl anything but welcoming.

Gus stepped forward, banging an overturned bucket with his toe. It tipped and grated against the cement walkway causing the horses behind him to neigh nervously. He grimaced and hurried to straighten the can before holding his hand out to the glowering stranger.

"Ah, sorry about that. I'm not usually so clumsy."

The man ignored his hand to yell at a couple of workers. "Bill, Fred, get those horses calmed down. What do you think Jorgenson pays you for?" His lips contorted, a shadow passing over his features, then he turned back to Gus. "What do you want?"

So he'd heard.

Not that Gus was surprised. Word of mouth always spread like wildfire. It would make his investigation tough. Hard to catch people out when they were guarding their emotions. An image of Rebecca staring at him with hurt green eyes came back to haunt him. He'd looked for her before leaving the main house, but she wasn't around, and neither was the irascible manservant. She'd been the same as he remembered. A little more cynical maybe. That was to be expected. They hadn't left on the best of terms. He'd have to tell the chief about her. It could compromise the case otherwise. Not that he thought for one instant she had anything to do with the murder. Not his Becky.

Not.

His.

And why that struck home like a knife to the gut, he wasn't about to analyze.

The man in front of him gave an impatient sigh and rubbed the back of his neck. Going by the way the men had jumped to do his bidding and the deep lines marring his forehead, Gus figured maybe all was not well in paradise. Even the rich and famous had their problems.

"Well, sir," he said, starting again. "I'm Detective Grant with the Chandler County Investigative Services. Based in Lexington, sir. We're here to investigate the death of Mr. Jorgenson." He hesitated a moment, but the other man's thoughts were buttoned down. "I imagine you've heard the bad news by now?"

The guy turned and walked back into his office,

leaving Gus to follow, or not. "I heard. What's that got to do with me?"

Gus took the invitation and entered the room. Immediately, he began to sneeze. Ha-choo. Ha-choo. He tugged out his handkerchief and wiped his nose and mouth. Ha-choo.

The guy sighed again and sank into his seat behind the desk. "Sounds like you're allergic to something, Detective. Maybe you should leave before it gets worse."

Gus shook his head. "Thanks, but I'm fine. It's probably a head cold." He wandered around the room, admiring the drawings of the various winning horses. "You do this...?"

"McMillon. Steve. And yeah, in my spare time I like to doodle."

Gus couldn't tell if he was being sarcastic, but decided to give him the benefit of the doubt. "You're pretty good. I should get you to draw my dog sometime." Then, before McMillon could come up with an adequate response, he added, "Not that you would, I know that, sir. I've been reading up on you."

McMillon stiffened. "What for?"

Gus smiled and picked up a curry comb, turning it over in his hands. "I like to know everything I can about a victim's family and friends."

He set the comb down and moved on to a short

whip looking thing, a crop he thought they were called. "It's a known fact that eight out of ten murders are committed by someone the victim knew, usually someone close." He stopped playing with the crop and stared at McMillon. "Interesting, don't you agree?"

Steve's hands were gripping the arms of his chair so hard there were bound to be dents. He shoved the chair back and rose to his feet.

"What the hell are you getting at?" He growled. "You can't think *I* had anything to do with Jorgenson's death?" He rounded the desk and took the crop out of Gus's hand. "I think you'd better leave."

Gus straightened, aware that he was at least six inches taller and fifty pounds lighter than the other man. "I'm just doing my job, Mr. McMillon. I understand you and Mr. Jorgenson didn't always agree on some aspects of care for the horses. You want to tell me about that here, or we can do it at the station. It's up to you."

The ruddiness of anger climbed McMillon's cheeks like fingerprints in sand. "I want a lawyer."

Gus nodded. He'd expected no less. "That's certainly within your right, of course. Too bad though."

Steve stared at him like he wanted to squash him like a bug. "What do you mean by that?"

Gus moved to the doorway, out of range of those ham hock fists. "Just that I had already crossed you off my list of suspects. I guess I jumped the gun." He turned to leave. "Please be at my office by noon tomorrow, Mr. McMillon. And bring your lawyer."

Gus walked down the long corridor and could feel the daggers nailing him in the back. That went well.

He sneezed again.

Chapter Seven

CHANDLER COUNTY

Rebecca hurried along Bourbonville's main street, her daughter on her hip. The witch had sent her on a list of errands today even though she knew little Sara hadn't been feeling well for the past couple of days. With everyone working over-time to prepare for the Derby—because Lord knows, they couldn't cancel, even though there had been a murder in the house—Jocelyn couldn't watch her as she normally did. The gentle cook had practically adopted her as a favorite niece and Sara loved spending time with her. Becky didn't know what she would have done without her friend. The stigma of becoming a single parent had cost her most of her friends and all of her family. But, she didn't regret having her beautiful baby girl for one moment. Sara made life worth living.

She pushed open the heavy glass door of the

Blooming Petals Flower Shop and sighed. Five people stood in line at the till and another four or five wandered the small shop waiting their turn. This was going to take forever. She didn't see why a phone call couldn't have got the job done, but Mrs. J had insisted. There was nothing for it, she was just going to have to wait.

She glanced at the baby resting on her shoulder. At least Sara had fallen asleep. She'd been fussy when they'd started out this morning. If it continued much longer, Becky would have to take her in to see the doctor, something she could ill afford. Especially since she could soon be out of a job. The rumors were flying now that Mr. Jorgenson was gone. Some thought the ranch would be put up for sale right after the Derby, hence the need to make everything perfect. Some of the other staff seemed to feel Mrs. J had always been the boss of Jorgensons and now she was setting out to prove it. Rebecca blinked away the ready tears. She just wanted everything to go back to the way it was before Mr. Jorgenson supposedly killed himself.

"Rebecca Hayes, is that you?" a shrill voice carried from the front of the store.

All eyes turned her way, leaving Becky pinned in place like a bug on a board. Her cheeks flared and she cursed her fair coloring as she searched the crowd for the blow horn caller.

A woman left the line, her swanky dress and perfectly coiffed head telling Rebecca who it was before she announced it for the benefit of the store.

"It's me, dear, Marnie Maples. Remember, we went to school together?" She swayed forward on three inch heels and a fitted black polka dot pencil dress. A matching bandanna, tied in a jaunty bow holding her blond curls away from her striking face, finished the ensemble.

Gus's ex-wife.

Of all the bad luck.

"Hello, Marnie," she said, giving in to the inevitable. "It's been a while."

The other woman eyed the baby in her arms and gave a sarcastic laugh. "I'll say. A lot has changed. Who's the lucky guy?"

Becky froze, her hand automatically covering Sara's head protectively. "No one you know." It was true. Marnie had never taken the time to appreciate the man she'd made her husband. They'd married right out of school and it hadn't taken long for things to fall apart. When Becky first met Gus, he'd been recovering from crushed pride more than a broken heart, but that didn't help with her jealousy. Marnie could be Marilyn Monroe's sister; it had intimidated the hell out of her.

"I heard a rumor that you're living on Balmoral, the Jorgenson spread." She held up the county newspaper, the Chandlerville Chronicles. The headline read; *Horse Entrepreneur Found Dead.* "It sounds as though you've had some excitement recently?"

The avid curiosity radiating as much from her periwinkle blue eyes as that of the other customers within listening range, made Becky inwardly cringe. Why did people always act like a pack of wolves when they sensed a weakness?

Sara seemed to pick up on her rising anxiety and moved fretfully, her chubby red cheeks warm against Becky's neck. She patted the baby's back, bouncing lightly on the balls of her feet while trying to pacify the hungry crowd.

"There's an ongoing investigation. I'm not at liberty to say anything about Mr. Jorgenson's death."

"So there *is* an investigation." The gleam in Marnie's eyes turned predatory. "And is my bumbling ex-husband involved?" She ran a blood-red nail along the stem of a snowy white rose. The fresh, earthy scent of the flower shop seemed to turn corrosive and pungent.

Becky gazed desperately toward the cash register, and was relieved to see a space had opened. She angled away from the angry vixen, smiling at the harried looking clerk. "Sorry, Marnie, I have to go. It's been really nice seeing you again." *Liar, liar, pants on fire.*

"Yes," Marnie chirped to her back. "We'll have to

get together and chat about the old days, sometime. I'd love to find out what my husband saw in you."

She didn't just say that.

Rebecca stopped dead in her tracks and swung around on one sneakered heel. "It was ex-husband, as you very well know, Marnie Maples. And we had lots in common. Like how much we detested overbearing, incredibly rude, females."

The crowd had formed a circle around the two women who stood like combatants in a ring, but if they were hoping for a fight they were doomed to disappointment.

Marnie jutted one elegant hip and smirked, her lips in their matching red gloss puckering in a little moue of amusement. "Hmm, so the kitten spits. Well, there's no need, darling. I gave him up first."

With that, she turned and strutted out the door like she was on a fashion show runway.

An elderly woman Becky faintly remembered as being the local veterinarian's wife stepped forward and held her arms out for Sara. "Let me take her while you do your business there." She nodded to the till. "Have six of my own and thirteen grandkids. Reckon I know how to hold one that's a-fussin'."

Rebecca hesitated, off-kilter thanks to that upsetting encounter. But she still needed to get Mrs. J's order in, so she smiled and kissed her baby before handing her over to the grandmotherly woman.

"If you're sure. I really appreciate this. She's been out of sorts for a few days now and very clingy. It makes it hard to get anything done."

The woman nodded her head, her hand brushing Sara's curls back from her forehead. "Oh, I know. These little ones don't take time into account. She does seem a trifle warm. Have you given her anything to ease the fever?"

"No," Rebecca said, embarrassed. "We haven't been to the doctor's office yet."

Mrs. Baker patted her hand. "Home remedies work just fine, love. Try a little Chamomile tea with honey and a cool bath. Little ones spike fevers and then they're gone. Don't get me wrong, you need to keep a close watch on her, but my guess is she'll be just fine in a day or two."

The other woman's calm practicality eased Becky's mind. With that many children, she was bound to know what she was talking about. "Thank you. I've been so worried."

"It's no problem at all, dear. Now, see to your order so you can get this young one home to bed." Mrs. Baker advised with a smile.

Rebecca turned back to the counter and pulled out the papers for the Derby after party, but her thoughts were on Marnie. Why did she want to know about Augustus? She'd seemed more worried about finding out where he was than the news of Mr. Jorgenson's death.

If she planned on getting Gus back, Becky wanted to be far, far away.

Chapter Eight

Doc Baker drove up the long, winding drive to the Jorgenson horse barns and ruminated on what would lead a man who seemed to have the world by the tail to take his life on the eve of the biggest day of his career. He'd only had a few conversations with the big man; most of his dealings were with the head trainer, Steve McMillon.

Now there was a guy with a boatload of stress. Good thing he had broad shoulders. Doc had known the man's father back in the day. He'd led three colts to wins in different legs of the Triple Crown, but had never reached the ultimate pinnacle of success. From what Doc had seen so far, the younger McMillon might just pull it off—if they could get Forever Humble back to health.

He pulled up to the main building and climbed out

of his aging Ford with its numerous creaks and groans. Sort of like him.

"Hey, Doc. Glad you could make it." Steve strode from the shadows of the wide double-door entry, Humble following on a long lead.

Doc put his arthritic hands on his hips and watched the colt as he lagged behind the trainer, nothing like the normal high-tempered prancing steps he usually exhibited.

"How long has he been like this?" he asked.

Steve stopped and rubbed the horse's forelock, brushing under the black bangs. "About a week now. It started out with him off his feed, but progressed to where I haven't been able to get him to eat anything for the last day and a half."

Doc grabbed his bag out of the box and eased his way over to the colt's good side, well aware of the strength in those legs.

"How you doin' there, fella?" He ran experienced hands over the animal's back, chest, stomach, and the front and back fetlocks, checking for soreness or swelling. Other than a couple flicks of the tail, Humble ignored him.

"See, Doc. Nothing." Steve's mouth turned down. "I don't get it."

With the Derby just shy of two weeks away, it was no wonder he was concerned. The race course demanded a clean bill of health on race day or the horse didn't run. Period, no exceptions. And since the Triple Crown was a three-year old's competition, this was it for Humble.

It was now or never.

Doc set his bag down and opened the colt's mouth, pressing lightly on the upper gums until the flesh turned light pinky-white. He released the pressure and watched to see how long before the color returned to normal.

Next he folded a piece of skin on the animal's chest, held for a minute, then released, and frowned at the resulting ridge. He tugged the stethoscope from his bag, placed the ends to his ears, and set it on the lower neck, listening to the shallow breaths and too-fast heartbeat. Lastly, he patted the horse's forelock and assessed the dull eyes that stared at him with such sad acceptance.

"Well, son," he said, meeting the younger man's worried gaze. "I'd like to draw some blood, just to rule out a couple of things, but near as I can tell your horse is suffering from dehydration."

McMillon stiffened. "What are you talking about, Doc? I check the stalls myself, every morning. The water is fresh."

Doc nodded. "I'm sure it is. Won't do no good if the horse doesn't drink it though." He dropped the stethoscope into the bag and came out with a small sample bag of rock salt. "Try this at his next feeding, it might help."

Steve turned the bag over in his hands, then looked up, brows lowered. "This is salt. I already have blocks out in each stall. This isn't my first rodeo, Doc."

Doc would've smiled if the man weren't so serious. "Some horses take funny notions. It can't hurt to give it a try, can it?" He gazed toward the big house, still and somber in the afternoon light. "Heard anything more on Mr. Jorgenson?"

He wasn't a gossiper, but if he didn't at least try to get some juicy tidbit his wife would never let him alone and 'Variety Playhouse' was on tonight, he didn't want to miss it.

McMillon glanced toward the house, and an indefinable look passed over his face. "Nah. The cops were here a couple of days ago, but they," he nodded toward the manor, "don't tell us nothin'."

A smidge of a bitter undertone there. Clearly, all was not well in Eden. "Rumor has it he was murdered." Doc drew the last vial of blood and closed his kit. He looked up and smiled. "You know how small towns are, everyone knows everyone else's business." Rather than easing the moment as he'd hoped, his words only seemed to anger the trainer.

"Yeah, well, if people spent more time minding

their own *business* maybe the world would be a better place," McMillon growled.

Slam. He could take a hint. Especially when it was practically rammed down his throat. He hefted his bag, gave the colt one last pat, and headed toward his truck. "I'll get back to you in a couple of days with the test results. Meanwhile, work on getting him hydrated, even if you have to bottle-feed him."

He slammed the door shut and started old Betsy with a cough and a chug, waved good-bye to McMillon's departing back, and sped down the drive.

Something bad was going on at the Jorgenson farm, and he had a feeling it was only going to get worse.

Chapter Nine

CHANDLER COUNTY

ugustus sat hunched over his desk, tie loosened and hair no doubt rumpled from all the scrunching he'd done to it after hours of research. His eyes felt square, The Chronicle's fine black print blurred and dancing on the page.

He leaned back and sighed. Time for a break. He'd been surprised by how often the Jorgenson name had appeared in back issues of the paper. They were treated like royalty around Bourbonville. Every move they made seemed to be newsworthy. Or at least the new Mrs. Jorgenson was. Helpful, if he didn't mind reading the society columns. She turned up almost weekly; hosting dinners at the country club, donating time and money to expand the theatre culture in the small town, parties at Balmoral, the list was endless. And through it all, there were black and white photos of her enamored, indulgent husband standing at her side.

Gus rubbed newsprint-stained fingers on one of his endless collection of handkerchiefs, grimacing at the gray blotches. He reached behind, lifted his suit jacket from the back of the chair, and shrugged into the tailored cotton coat. His stomach rumbled telling him it was hungry. Time to head over to Sadie's Café for lunch.

The sun was warm so he decided to give his legs a stretch and walk the few blocks to the restaurant. A large weeping cherry tree in front of the library reminded him of the Lexington Cemetery, beautiful at any time of year, but it was enough to steal your breath in the spring. Daffodils waved cheery golden heads as he passed by, and bees buzzed lazily from flower to flower enjoying the ripe bounty.

He passed the Bourbonville Fields, home to the local baseball organization, and currently the location for the upcoming carnival. Held the weekend before the Derby, volunteers were busy erecting tents for the 4-H competitions, pie-eating contests—his favorite—a barbecue rib cook-off, baking competitions, and even one with a wooden dance floor for the evening festivities. Soon the rides and carnival games would arrive and parents would dole out hard-earned cash for their children to enjoy this once a year event. Teen boys could test their oats by inviting a date and then showing off their prowess at the ring toss or dart throwing, and if they were lucky, they'd win a giant stuffed animal to cart around for the rest of the night—to their girlfriends' delight.

Gus smiled, though his heart gave a soft pang. He'd been that kid once, on a magical night he'd never forgotten. If only there was a way to go back...

He turned the corner onto Main Street and was just about to cross over to Sadie's when he saw a familiar figure leaving the flower shop, a young child in her arms.

Rebecca.

He hurried down the walk, drawn to her side like a lodestone. "Becky, wait," he called, not caring if he drew attention.

Startled, she spun and searched for the voice, her arm holding the toddler close. A complex mix of emotions chased across her face, and Gus wondered what she was thinking. There was a time he would've known.

"Augustus. How are you?" She smiled, composed now.

He was surprised by how much he missed the old, impulsive Rebecca.

"Hungry." He laughed, inviting her to relax and not go running off as her body language seemed to state with her hunched shoulders and fidgeting feet. She looked upset. "I was just heading over to Sadie's. Care to join me?"

She rubbed the child's back and kissed her downy cheek. "I can't. I should get home. Mrs. Jorgenson needs me."

His chest tightened. The baby looked like an extension of her body. She'd make a great mother.

"I wasn't aware the Jorgensons had any children," he murmured, a growing premonition turning his blood cold.

Her gaze was defiant. "She's mine, Gus. I had her two and a half years ago, right here in Bourbonville."

The ground shifted like quicksand. He felt like he was having an out-of-body experience. It was too great a coincidence.

The child was his.

"Why didn't you tell me?" His voice was little more than a guttural croak. He tried, but it was impossible to see himself in the dark curly cue hair, or chubby body and rosebud cheeks.

"What was there to say?" she demanded, lowering her tone when the baby fussed. "Would you have come back if I begged? Would you have been happy?"

He stood there, shocked. This was unbelievable. While he'd been off living his dream, she'd been here. Having. His. Baby.

Becky sighed. "It doesn't matter anymore. Thanks to the Jorgensons we're doing fine." She shifted the girl a little higher and stared at him as though she expected him to thank her or something. When he didn't, she turned away. "I gotta go."

Augustus watched her leave, her back ramrod straight, and knew he'd hurt her, but then she'd knocked the breath out of him, so they were even.

"Becky, wait," he called, relieved when she slowed to hear his words. He held his hand out in supplication. "Please, I don't even know her name. Come have lunch with me. We need to talk about this." He frowned at a couple of nosy pedestrians who stopped to hear her answer.

She hesitated, then gave a short nod. "It's Sara. You're right, we do. But not now." She glanced over her shoulder, her gaze cool, direct. "You know where I'm staying. See if you can find the time to come out there. You know, when you're not off saving the world."

With that parting shot she hurried away, leaving him standing on a busy street corner feeling like he was all alone.

Chapter Ten

S adie's was busy, the morning crowd giving way to the hectic lunch mob. Gus was about to leave without finding a table, his hunger a thing of the past anyway, when a voice he could have gone without hearing called his name.

Marnie.

His ex-wife looked as expertly turned out as ever. Tempted to pretend he hadn't heard her summons, he sighed and made his way through the throng to her booth. She leaned over and bussed his cheek—her expensive perfume making his eyes water —then slid onto the red and white trimmed leatherette seat and crossed silken legs in a measured move guaranteed to drive a man crazy. But not him. Not anymore.

"Hello, Augustus. I didn't know you were in town."

Her cherry red lips pursed in an amused smile. "Aren't you going to sit down?"

And here he was without his viper repellant.

Gus scrunched his lanky frame onto the bench across from her, taking care he didn't knock her knees. Music from a jukebox in the corner competed with the laughter and voices of happy customers and the tantalizing scents of bacon and fried onions.

A harried-looking waitress, a blue smear staining her white apron, came by with the coffee pot and filled his cup on the fly.

"Be back in a minute. Special's Southern Fried Steak with mashed potatoes and corn on the cob, or you can check out the menu there behind the napkin holder." She made a little pop with the gum in her mouth and then she was gone, a woman on a mission.

Gus grinned, relaxing after the tense exchange with Rebecca. That is until his gaze came back around to Marnie. She sat against the back of the booth, arms folded, and one long, red nail tapping out the Morse Code on the bright white teeth he'd paid for.

He raised a brow. "Cat got your tongue?"

She laughed, a light little tinkle he used to think was cute, but he now knew it meant she was up to something. "Just wondering what it is that could have brought the great Detective Augustus Grant back to our humble little town, that's all."

He hated when she mocked him. Which, of course, is the reason she did it.

"I've been called in to investigate a murder. But then, I'm sure you already know this," he said, calmly enough. It never paid to give her any ammunition. She was adept at turning the simplest words into open warfare.

"Ah, yes, the Jorgenson heir. Poor man. He really had no luck, did he?"

Rather than looking suitably saddened by the death, she almost glowed with excitement. He knew it, she was up to something. Not willing to play her game, he reached for the sugar container and carefully measured two level spoons into his coffee, then added the same amount of milk from a little white porcelain carafe. He stirred the mixture clockwise two times, then counter-clockwise once before setting the spoon aside and lifting the cup to his lips. He took a sip and sighed his contentment, listening to the rise and fall of the conversations around them. If only everything in life could be settled with coffee.

"You never change," Marnie said, and he didn't think it was meant as a compliment.

He shrugged. "Routines are good for the soul."

"And boring as hell," she retorted.

His turn to smile. "Good thing we got a divorce

then, isn't it?" They should never have married in the first place.

"You sound bitter, darling." She waved an elegant hand in the air. "Let's not fight, it's all old hat anyway." Her cornflower blue gaze turned sly. "You'll never guess who I ran into."

Oh, yes, he could.

Marnie hadn't wanted him for herself, but she wasn't willing to let him go, either. When their marriage fell apart—his fault as much as hers—she'd made it her job to sabotage his relationship with Rebecca. If only he'd known sooner.

The waitress breezed up to their table, notepad in hand. "Whatcha gonna have, sugar?" She held her pen poised, and glanced impatiently from Marnie to him.

"The special, please. No gravy, and easy on the potatoes." Gus gave her his friendliest smile. He had a feeling his ex-wife hadn't been making this poor woman's life easy. A guess proven with her next words.

"This water is still not hot enough." Marnie gave the squat Brown Betty teapot on its saucer a push towards the edge of the table. "How hard is it to boil water for pete's sake?"

The waitress sighed and popped her gum before picking up the pot. "I'm sorry, I thought all that steam and those bubbles said that it was ready. Guess I was wrong. Are you planning to order now?" *Or drive me crazy?*

Gus could practically hear her thoughts. He didn't blame her either. Marnie's attitude to those she considered beneath her was enough to drive a saint away from the church.

"I'll have a toasted tomato and lettuce sandwich. And for God's sake, go light on the mayonnaise this time. I swear, you all think mayonnaise is a staple around here." She waved the woman away, done now that she'd placed her order.

Gus shrugged and shared a commiserating look with the waitress that seemed to say, *What in the world are you doing with her?*

He was beginning to wonder the same thing.

"So," Marnie pouted, making sure he noticed her blood red lips. "Aren't you going to guess?"

Not on your life. There was no way he was falling into that trap. "Why don't you just tell me?"

She flounced back in her seat, no doubt frustrated he'd ruined her game. "I was in that dingy little flower shop down the street, you remember the one?" She waited for his nod. How could he forget? Half his damn pay check had gone into her penchant for fresh bouquets.

"And?" He tried to hurry her along, hoping she'd get annoyed and drop the topic.

No such luck.

"I ran into an old school chum. You might remember her, Rebecca Hayes?"

His stomach dropped into his shoes. Why didn't he just go back to the office instead of insisting everything was normal, when in fact his world had just imploded.

He tried to act nonchalant, lifting his cup and taking a sip of his coffee, only to find it was too hot and he burned his tongue. He met his wife's—ex-wife's—satisfied expression over the rim of the cup and sighed. "Make your point, my dear. I need to get back to work soon."

Their meals arrived. His was a heaping plate fit for a lumberjack. He lifted his fork and forced himself to take a bite of the fragrant garlic mashed potatoes, though thanks to the company, it tasted like sawdust.

She frowned, one elegant eyebrow lowering in annoyance. "Don't you even care that I know about your torrid affair?" She barely glanced at her own sandwich, just pushed the plate aside. "She has a baby, Gus."

This was his day for enlightening conversations apparently. He set his fork down and used a paper napkin to carefully wipe his mouth, then folded it into a precise square before setting it under his cup as a coaster.

Finally, he looked up and met her irritated gaze. "It

wasn't an affair, as you very well know. And yes, I am aware of the child. That is between myself and Rebecca. Stay out of it, Marnie."

It wasn't often that he made a demand and it seemed to confound her.

"Whatever do you mean?" she asked. "I thought you would be happy for her. After all, the Jorgensons are filthy rich. She'll never want for another thing."

Gus shook his head, sure that he'd misheard. "I don't understand...?" There was a painful ringing in his ears and the room had started to spin around him. Maybe he was coming down with something.

"The baby, you doofus." She laughed. "Your old girlfriend gave birth to the next Jorgenson heir."

He stared across the table into her victorious face and felt his whole world slip off its axis for the second time in one day.

Rebecca had lied to him.

Chapter Eleven

Becky stumbled through the back door of the big house, her hands loaded with bags of fabric and lace, Mrs. J's Pall Malls, and Sara.

Jocelyn turned from the sink and hurried to help, her bell skirts sweeping the ceramic tiles of the kitchen. "Gracious, child. What have you got there?"

Becky gratefully handed the baby over to her friend and dropped the rest of the parcels onto the table, sighing her relief. She smiled as Sara burst out giggling thanks to Jocelyn's busy fingers tickling her chubby tummy and legs. There was no sweeter sound than that of a happy child.

"Thanks. Those bags were getting heavy."

Jocelyn plunked herself down on a chair and settled the baby in her lap, handing over a teaspoon to keep her occupied. "I don't see why you have to go chasing around the countryside for the witch. Let her go and get her own chores done."

Rebecca wandered over to the counter and spied a freshly made pineapple upside down cake. Her stomach gurgled, reminding her she'd missed out on lunch. "Mind if I have a slice?" she asked, glancing over her shoulder.

Jocelyn waved her hand in the air. "Of course you can. It'll just be hitting the garbage anyhow. You know how Mrs. Jorgenson is about dessert."

And about dust. And about noise. And about... the list was endless. Now that Mr. Jorgenson was gone, Becky feared their days on the ranch were numbered. Mrs. J was a city girl and often spent days in Lexington, only returning to Bourbonville when her money ran low. The staff knew to stay out of her way when that happened; she was like a tiger with its tail caught in a trap. Dangerous.

She moaned around the first bite of cake. The brown sugar and pineapple melted on her tongue with sugary goodness. Jocelyn was an amazing cook. Even if they did have to find new jobs, she'd be fine. Sadie's had tried to hire her more than once already, and had a standing weekly order for fresh fruit pies.

But, what about her and Sara?

What would they do without the security of Balmoral? She looked at her happy baby and swallowed sudden tears. Why, oh, why did Mr. Jorgenson make the truly awful decision to take his life?

"Momma, Momma," Sara chirped, her arms out like a mini-Frankenstein as she lurched across the kitchen, her eyes on the forgotten cake.

Rebecca swooped down and swung her daughter around before giving her a big, smacking kiss on the cheek. "Where do you think you're going, missy?"

"Cake," Sara demanded. "Cake." Her blue eyes, so startling against the dark curliness of her hair and creamy complexion, sparkled with laughter.

Becky took a little on the end of the fork and fed it through the rosebud lips. "Yes, cake. Good girl."

Sara was growing so fast. Just a few months ago she'd still been crawling. Now she was a walking, talking trouble magnet. Like her father, Sara was clumsy and not happy unless she was into something. Yesterday, she'd given Rebecca a heart attack by disappearing between one instant and the next. They'd been outside, taking advantage of the beautiful spring day while Becky worked on some new runners for the dining room table. She'd set Sara in the thick blue-green Kentucky grass to play and when she looked up, her daughter was gone.

A frantic search later, Emmett, Jocelyn's husband, found her wandering toward the horse pens chanting, "Horsey, horsey." Becky's heart still hurt thinking about it.

"She's alearning a new word every day," Jocelyn said, a wistful look in her dark chocolate eyes.

Becky gave Sara another bite, then set her down to wander the relative safety of the big kitchen. "Emmett still not ready for children?" Her friend had been dreaming of a big family since high school.

"Nah, you knows what he says, 'Not 'til we can afford a home of our own.' Darn male pride. We'll be old enough to be grandparents by the time we can ever have us some kids."

Rebecca wished there was something she could do to help, but she was barely maintaining as it was. The Jorgensons had left the household income expenses to their trusted manservant, Ernest, and that man knew how to squeeze every drop of labor out of a nickel. Unfortunately, with the economy struggling to regain its footing after the end of World War II, there were not a lot of choices for an unwed mother. She considered herself fortunate to have received this position, thanks to Jocelyn.

She leaned over and gave her friend a hug, breathing in the homey scents of vanilla and yeast from the bread she made every morning. "Don't give up," she whispered.

Jocelyn wiped away the tears gathering in the corners of her eyes and gave a shaky smile. "You know me, I keep my faith close." She tugged Rebecca onto the chair beside her. "Enough about me. What news did you hear whilst you was in town? Any more about Mr. J?"

Even though they lived in the same house, the staff had no idea how the investigation into his death was progressing. Nothing but rumors. The most salient one being that he'd been murdered.

Augustus sprang to mind, along with his shocked anger at finding she'd kept his daughter a secret from him. A quiver of fear mixed with the thrill of seeing him again, ran up her spine. She looked into Jocelyn's curious coffee-colored eyes and tried to smile. "No, nothing about Mr. Jorgenson, but I did run into Gus."

Jocelyn stiffened, full of righteous indignation. "What did *he* want?" she snapped, then glanced at the startled Sara who sat on the floor amid a pile of pots and stared at them with eyes grown saucer-wide. She grasped Becky's hand and squeezed. "He done give up his rights to that chil', don't you go taking no guff from him."

She'd never forgiven Gus for walking out on

Rebecca, even though Becky had tried to tell her it was just as much her fault as his. If he'd known about the baby, he'd never have left to better his career, she knew that. And it would have festered until it destroyed them. At least this way, it was a clean break. Or it had been.

Until he came back.

Chapter Twelve

E mmett fidgeted, his nerves on edge as he scanned the empty corridor of the long barn. *Where was he?*

Any moment, someone was gonna walk on in and he'd have some fancy explainin' to do. He shoulda been down at the track an hour ago. It was too dangerous to be doing this now, so close to the Derby. He'd warned them, but they wouldn't listen.

Nobody listened to ol' Emmett.

The door creaked open, allowing a stream of light to filter in and catch the hay particles floating lazily in the air.

"You there?" a voice shouted—at least it seemed that way to Emmett.

He hurried forward, careful to keep on the

shadowy side of the row. "Hush. What are you trying to do, get me done killed?"

Sheriff Tromley stepped into the opening, the badge gleaming dully on his crisp tan shirt. A stalk of hay waved casually from the corner of his mouth. "Relax. We're just a couple of friends having a chat. Nothing wrong with that, now is there?"

Nothing, except he was a white lawman while Emmett... wasn't.

"Look, I ain't heard nothing, okay?" He glanced over the sheriff's shoulder and wished he'd never taken that first bribe. "I gotta get going."

He attempted to pass the lawman, escape only a few short paces away, but a hard, black baton blocked his path. He froze and sucked in a shaky breath.

"Not so fast there, *boy*." The sheriff nudged him backward into one of the empty stalls. "You and I aren't done conversating yet. I just hate rude people." He slammed the end of the stick into Emmett's gut, causing him to fold in on himself, the breath forced from his body. "Don't you?"

Wheezing through the pain, Emmett eyed Tromley as he wandered the perimeter of the pen, stopping to grab a handful of feed from the trough and let it trickle through his fingers like grains of sand in an hourglass. That's how Emmett felt; his fate flowed uncontrollably through a hole he couldn't plug.

"How's Forever Humble?" Tromley asked, the question innocuous enough to anyone passing by.

Emmett wiped the spittle from his lips and straightened, careful not to show weakness though his ribs hurt like a son-of-a-gun. "Doc came by a couple a'days ago to check him over; he's been off his feed." He spared a sardonic glance at the grain in the sheriff's hand. "Figured it to be dehydration. Nothing to worry about."

Tromley let go of the rest of the seed, pulled a snowy white handkerchief from his pocket, and wiped his hands slowly and carefully. He looked up and smiled. "That's good. Real good. We don't want anything happening to the Bourbonville favorite, now do we?"

He tapped the baton against a meaty thigh and strode to the door of the stall. It opened on near-silent hinges that still managed to send a shiver down Emmett's spine.

The sheriff plucked the straw from his lips and let it drop to the ground where he deliberately crushed it under the pointy toe of his cowboy boot.

"Slow and easy. Just keep to the plan and your pretty little wife can continue to use her handy fingers to cook you those pies. You hear me, *boy*?"

Emmett stood in the center of the horse stall with a thin patch of morning light doing nothing to warm his

chilled skin until long after Sheriff Tromley's departure. They'd probably hang him, but if that man came
near his Jocelyn, he would surely kill him.

So help him, God, he would.

Chapter Thirteen

CHANDLER COUNTY

By the time Gus shook himself clear of his ex-wife and returned to the station, it was already mid-afternoon. He'd intended to go down to the racetrack and question some of the locals on their impressions about John Jorgenson's state of mind during the past few weeks, but it looked as though that would have to wait. Most trainers preferred to run their horses during the morning, before the temperature rose and the reporters arrived to stir up trouble.

He also wanted to drive out to Balmoral and confront Rebecca. How could she tell him such a treasonous lie, and why? What did she hope to accomplish? If the baby really was Jorgenson's, she'd be better off going to see a lawyer to protect the child's assets.

And if it was his...

If the baby was his, he planned on doing something about it. He just wasn't sure what. He'd never thought much about children, even when he'd been married—especially then. Marnie was about the furthest from a motherly type person you could get. But, Rebecca... she was different. Kind and caring. Loving and nurturing. Unfamiliar joy coursed through his veins. Seeing her today, holding that child—it had filled him with a yearning for what they had lost. What he had walked away from.

If only he'd known.

And that was his answer. Rebecca hadn't lied. She wasn't made that way, while the same could not be said for Marnie. His shoulders sagged. He'd once again been a pawn in one of his ex-wife's silly little games. The good news was he'd figured it out before accusing Becky of something she hadn't done. The bad news—he was a father and he didn't know the first thing about being one. His own dad had been a drunk, a mean one. His mom had tried, but after a while it became too much and she'd taken her life. All of which created a strong will to protect the innocent.

Rebecca hadn't understood. They'd argued. She'd been determined to create a sanctuary for them right there in Bourbonville, and he'd felt the lure of adventure. The chance to make a difference. So, he'd gone on his quest, and succeeded for the most part.

THE LADY SAID NO

But, he'd never forgotten the girl he'd left behind.

Rebecca Hayes.

"You gonna stand there moonin' all day, or are you opening the door?"

The sarcastic voice startled Gus out of his thoughts. He glanced over his shoulder to see the sheriff climbing the stairs, his hat tipped back on his head like a good ol' farm boy. The faint aroma of dung clung to the air and Gus's nose crinkled. "Where have you been?"

Tromley grinned. "What's the matter, Detective? City life turning you into a pansy?"

Gus refrained from saying what he was thinking, which was the dung had certainly attached itself to the right ass. He tugged open the door and stepped into the two-man office that constituted the police department for Bourbonville. The big cases were sent over to Chandlerville, thirty miles away, and if necessary they could call in help from Lexington. So far, the Jorgenson case remained in their jurisdiction. Gus didn't know how long that would last if what he suspected was true and the man had been murdered.

"When are you heading back to Lexington? This case is cut and dried, Augustus." The sheriff crossed the entry to his office and sank into his worn leather desk chair, stretched out his legs, and crossed his feet at the ankle. "Even us hillbillies know how to fill in a suicide report."

We don't need you here.

The words were unsaid but just as clear as if he'd shouted them. Tromley wanted him gone. The question was why.

"You been out to the Jorgenson estate this morning, Sheriff?" Gus searched the counter for a halfway clean mug, then poured himself a cup of the pitch black coffee that had been resting on the back of the Franklin stove sitting in the corner of the room. He took a drink and shivered as the rotgut worked its way down his throat.

Tromley straightened, a frown marring his classically handsome face. "Why do you ask?"

"Well, sir," Gus said, offering him the pot and setting it down when the other man shook his head. "There was the, um, outdoorsy scent that I mentioned earlier, but..." He pointed at the fancy leather cowboy boots planted on the floor. "I noticed your boots had straw caught in the heel. Figured it had to come from a barn, and the logical assumption from all that was the Jorgenson place." He smiled into his cup. "Guess I was right."

Tromley looked at his boot, where sure enough, a few pieces of straw had wedged between his heel and the sole of his shoe. He regarded Gus through narrowed eyes. "What kind of game are you playing, Detective? There ain't no law that says I can't go for a walk through a dad-blasted field, now is there?"

Gus strode over to his temporary desk and checked for any messages the secretary might have left before she finished her job for the day. There was one from his commanding officer warning him to wrap things up soon, and another from the president's security detail. Ever since he'd saved the man's daughter, they'd been after him to give up police work and join the unit in D.C. He couldn't see himself as a glorified babysitter, but the offer was tempting. A new car, new house, plenty of travel. And doing something he loved, protecting the innocent.

"No," he murmured, and tapped his cheek thoughtfully. "I was just wondering, sir. What makes a guy like you, wearing fancy boots like those," he nodded at the footwear in question, "go for a walk through a pasture full of horse manure?" His nose wrinkled again.

A thundercloud appeared behind the sheriff's normally placid expression. He shoved the chair back and stormed to the door, opening it so hard it smacked the wall and left a small gouge in the plaster. "What I do in my own town ain't none of your damn business, Grant. Finish what it is you came here to do and give me back my office." He stomped down the stairs, leaving the door wide open.

Gus watched as he climbed into the patrol car and sped off down the street like the hounds of hell were after him.

Oh, he planned on finishing, all right. And catch a killer in the process.

Chapter Fourteen

I t was two days before Gus had another chance to drive out to the Balmoral estate. He'd been down to the race track the morning before, but hadn't learned much of interest. The horse community had closed ranks. They may not have approved of Jorgenson, but they weren't about to give up the dirt on him either.

The sky was an impossible blue, without a cloud in sight. Days like this, it was hard to imagine evil existed, but Gus knew it did. He'd seen his share of wrongdoings. Some were crimes of opportunity, but it was the murders driven by passion that got to him the most. Sad that a split-second decision could change everything. Not just for the killer or his victim, but everyone involved. Gus had found over the years he gained the most information from those on the outer perimeter of the crime. Friends of the friends, cleaning staff, groundskeepers, anyone not directly involved with the family in question. They didn't carry the same loyalty as those in the inner circle. Which is the reason he was on his way to interrogate Rebecca Hayes today.

Or so he told himself.

An older Ford pickup crested the hill in front of him, its chrome grill piercing his eyes from the sun's reflection. Gus pulled over to the side of the gravel drive to let it by, then realized it was the veterinarian from town. He honked his horn and waved out his window for him to stop.

The truck rolled to a halt and a gray head poked out of the cab. "Trouble there, son?"

Gus grinned. He hadn't been called a youngster in a good many years. "No, sir," he answered, holding his arm across the distance for a handshake. "You wouldn't happen to be the Jorgensons' vet, now would ya?"

The man pulled his hand back and judged him from beneath bushy salt and pepper eyebrows. "I *am* the county veterinarian, yes. Who's asking?"

Gus turned on his best aw-shucks smile and held up his badge. "Detective Augustus Grant. Sorry, sir, I didn't mean no disrespect. I was hoping you could tell me what you know about the Jorgenson family. Do you have any idea who their enemies might be?"

The vet put gnarled hands on the steering wheel and shook his head. "No idea. Are you saying Mr. Jorgenson didn't...?" His Adam's apple bobbed.

Funny. He must have seen a hundred sick or dying critters in his lifetime, but the thought of a human's death turned the man pea-green. Or, was it *this* human's death?

"Can you tell me where you were on the night of April fifteenth, approximately between eight p.m. and midnight, Doctor?"

The fingers gripping the steering wheel shook. "Well, I can't rightly say. Most likely at home on the couch after one of my wife's dinners." He frowned. "No, wait. That was the night the Robinsons' mare gave birth. She's young and was having a tough go so they called me out. I was there until two or three in the morning, that little cuss wasn't in any hurry to greet the world." He smiled, but then it slid sideways. "Are you accusing me of murder, young man?"

The way he said it Gus thought he was about to get a whopping. He liked this old codger. "No, sir. I wouldn't dream of it. Just trying to keep my facts straight, you know how it is." Hoping he'd get further with a little give and take, he leaned out his window. "Truth is, this case is getting the best of me. We have a dead man... pardon me, sir," he muttered when the Doc stiffened. "Mr. Jorgenson has passed on and we have no real suspects. That's what I was hoping you could help me with." He waved his hand in a circular motion. "Since you take care of those fine animals, and all."

They both stared through Doc's passenger window as a group of five horses, two with foals, pranced by the fence.

Doc sighed, his shoulders bowing as though under a tremendous weight. "I knew something was going on. I just knew it."

Gus held his breath, his target was treading the line. Too hard a tug and he'd lose him. "Mind explaining that, sir?"

The Doctor reached over and turned off his truck. As it hiccupped into silence, he picked up a sheaf of papers from the seat beside him and handed them to Gus. "I was out a few days ago to check on Humble— Forever Humble, the colt the Jorgensons have entered into the Derby?" he clarified. "Anyway, the poor thing was severely dehydrated, and off his feed. I drew blood for some tests... those there are the results."

Gus stared at the older man for a moment and detected a heartfelt sadness that told him more than the words on the page ever could. He gave a short nod of thanks and tried to figure out what it was he was reading.

"If I've got this right, it looks as though someone

gave this horse a diuretic?" He tapped the pages and looked to the doc for confirmation.

The other man shook his head. "It's not that simple. You give a horse stuff like that there to increase his stamina. It flushes up to two percent of the animal's weight in water and upsets his electrolyte balance. The loss of all that water, which can equal several gallons, gives the horse a weight handicap." He ran a tired hand through his hair. "It could make the difference on a win. But it can also kill him, son."

Gus sat back and contemplated the information. Why would anyone want to do something so horrendous to a defenseless animal? Unfortunately, he knew the answer. Money. The root of all evil.

"I thank you, sir. Mind if I hang onto these for a little while?" He held up the papers.

Doc hesitated, then shrugged. "They won't do you no good. It's not illegal to drug your horse, more's the shame." He started his truck. "Are we done? The wife should have my dinner sitting on the table. She gets right testy if I'm late."

Gus smiled, his heart giving a pang. He'd be making his own supper when he got home, and there wouldn't be anyone to share his day with either. "You bet. Thanks for your time, Doc. If I think of anything else, I'll get hold of you."

The doctor raised his hand and drove off, leaving Gus staring at a lonely dirt road.

Chapter Fifteen

The den had been carefully cleaned, every particle of chalk dust and blood stains removed so that the average onlooker would never know a man had died.

But she knew.

Even now the startled, pained look in his eyes the second after the bullet entered his brain lived on, filling every corner of the room with his presence.

It had taken all this time to build up the courage to enter. His spirit chased hers through her dreams. She had a very real fear she would never be rid of him.

But she was even more frightened by the monster who had killed him.

Her lover.

It was because of him she was here now; otherwise she would never have come near the place again. He wanted her to find the statue he'd bashed over John's head. He was concerned about the prints. Prints. Not the fact that he'd cold-bloodedly killed a man in his own home. No, he was worried about some bloody fingerprints. It boggled her mind.

She slipped around the perimeter of the room, gliding past row upon row of hard-bound books of every description—John had been proud of his collection of first editions—and the ornate cast iron pot belly stove he'd preferred to spend his evenings in front of, averting her eyes from the tufted leather chair he'd favored. She could still see him, a glass of bourbon in his hand and plaid slippers on his narrow feet.

The desk loomed large, a mahogany and brass centerpiece to an already ostentatious room. She searched its broad surface, but there was no sign of the statue she remembered seeing there.

Heart pounding, she whirled, her gaze combing the dim reaches of the room. It was gone. What was she supposed to do? Just as panic took hold, tightening its grip on her throat until she could barely breathe, she saw it. The statue.

It had been moved and now sat on the console table under the bay window. She hurried across the room, stomach churning. Any moment she expected someone to come through that door and raise the alarm.

The sculpture seemed smaller than the one she

remembered, and where was the spear? This figurine was of a cowboy getting bucked off a horse, a rattlesnake thrashing at its feet. How appropriate. There was no choice; he'd demanded she find the ornament and this was the only one here.

Maybe he wouldn't notice.

She lifted the cool bronze, grimacing at the surprising weight of the object, and stuffed it into her oversized handbag. She hefted it onto her shoulder and was about to leave the room when a plume of dust from outside caught her attention. A white convertible pulled into the yard, the top up and the glare on the glass stopping her from seeing who was inside until he stepped out of the car.

The detective.

She froze.

Her heart beat like a wild thing in her chest, her body going into full flight mode. She tightened her grip on the handbag, caught between leaving the statue behind and attempting to escape without being seen. If only this room didn't open into the Grand Hall.

He looked up, searching the windows as though sensing her gaze. There was nothing for it, he'd be in the house within moments.

She had to get out.

The bell rang at the same time as that stupid cuckoo clock behind the desk pealed, almost giving her heart palpitations. She carefully opened the door and peeked out, relieved to find the area empty. Not wasting another moment, she sped to the stairs and practically levitated, her adrenaline so high she never even noticed the heavy weight of the bag.

Just as she reached the top, she glanced down and sucked in a sharp breath.

Ernest stood at the bottom, his dark-eyed gaze boring a hole in her chest.

She straightened her spine, forced a sardonic smile that wasn't reciprocated, and with one hand clutching her purse—possibly the only thing between her and a grisly death—walked sedately down the hall to her room.

Chapter Sixteen

CHANDLER COUNTY

Gus rang the ornate brass doorbell and listened as the gong resounded on the other side of the twin oak doors. He reached up to tidy his windblown hair, then frowned. He wasn't here to impress anyone. It didn't stop him from straightening his tie and clearing his throat however.

He was just lifting his hand to punch the bell again when the door slid open a couple of unfriendly inches.

The butler filled the gap, his coal-dark eyes reserved. "Yes?"

Gus blinked. "Ah, hello. Detective Grant, I was here last week?"

No reaction. The man didn't even blink.

"I ah, was wondering if I could ask Mrs. Jorgenson a few more questions. It won't take long." Gus was tempted to put his foot in the door, but suspected it wouldn't stop the manservant from slamming it closed.

"She's unavailable," the man said, a hint of satisfaction in his tone.

Gus glanced down at his wrist watch. He'd promised the commander he would drive to Lexington and give him an update on the case. He'd just have to return to the ranch another day. He rummaged around the pocket of his trench coat and came up with the brass business card case he'd been given the day he passed the academy.

"Can you..." The words dried in his throat as his gaze skimmed over the butler's shoulder and landed on the slim legs encased in a bright blue pair of stovepipe pants visible at the top of the staircase. A shapely body in a boxy white shirt glided down the steps and revealed what his heart already knew—Rebecca.

"What are you doing here, Gus?" Her tobacco brown hair, done up in a high ponytail that reminded him of high school, swung back and forth as she moved, a reflection of her disapproval.

The butler, Ernest, turned at the sound of her voice, a look passing over his face like a shadow that gave Gus pause. What was that about?

"Gus?" she repeated, half impatient, half resigned. She stopped on the last tread, a foot on the hard wood flooring and her hand resting on the newel post. Gus wished he had his camera with him. She'd always been photogenic, but now, with a little more maturity to her features she'd become breathtaking.

"He was just leaving," Ernest said, adding weight to the door.

Gus put out a hand to stop it closing in his face. "I needed to talk to the missus," he admitted, and couldn't deny the momentary triumph at her crestfallen expression. "But I was hoping to see you more." He ignored the exasperated manservant and used the only hook he had. "It's about Mr. Jorgenson."

She got a deer in the headlights look that immediately sent up a dozen red flags. What the heck had she gotten herself into?

"C'mon, Becky. It'll only take a moment."

Ernest stepped between them, his shoulder connecting with the door now. "Miss Hayes has a job, Detective. Come back when the mistress is home. Good day."

The door creaked as it started to close and Gus had no choice but to let go.

"Wait," Becky called, and he could hear her footsteps rushing across the floor. "Let him in, Ernest, for goodness sake."

Her pink-tipped fingers wrapped around the door jamb and there was a short tug-of-war before the butler gave an irritated sigh and moved out of the way.

And then she was there.

Her emerald green eyes left him breathless while her compact body revved everything inside him into overdrive. She'd tinged her lips with the same delicate pink as her nails and all he could think about was if it would smudge when he kissed her. Because if he got half the chance...

"Okay, I'm here. Start talking." She stood, one hand on her hip and the other on the door, effectively barring him entry into her world.

It annoyed him even as it turned him on. What happened to the sweet and biddable girl he'd left behind? This woman was confident, determined, and hotter than the Kentucky sun. But he couldn't forget the secret she'd kept from him. He was a father.

"Where's the...?" He stumbled to a halt.

She looked puzzled for a moment, then annoyed. Well, join the club.

"Baby, Gus. You can say it, can't you?" She sighed and stepped back. "You may as well come in. We'll have to sort this out sooner or later."

She waited until he stepped over the threshold—without stumbling for once—then closed the door and led the way down the hall toward the kitchen without so much as a glance back. Gus hesitated, scanning the entrance for the taciturn Ernest, but the man had disappeared, so he hurried to follow Becky's curvaceous butt.

Much like the first time he'd been here, the kitchen smelled of fresh baking, cinnamon rolls if he wasn't mistaken, with the underlying aroma of a roast in the oven. Gus's taste buds began to weep for joy.

The cook turned from peeling potatoes, a wicked looking knife in her hand and a lethal glint in her eyes. "What he be doin' here?"

Guess he wouldn't be trying those buns out then. Obviously, she was Rebecca's friend. Rather than getting upset, Gus was grateful to the woman. He could imagine how tough it would be as a single parent, what with the bias of the townspeople. Women had gained some respect since their invaluable contributions during the war, but many men remained close-minded and expected them to be like June Cleaver—make sure dinner was ready and the house clean.

"Mama, up," a demanding little voice chirped.

Gus spun toward the sound in time to see Rebecca bending at the waist, stretching those baby blue pants over a heart-shaped derriere to lift a toddler into her arms. The youngster wrapped pudgy arms around her mom's neck and peeked at him over her shoulder.

A girl.

He had a baby girl.

His heart expanded until he could barely breathe.

She was perfect. A tiny angel with curly dark hair and his eyes.

"What's her name?" he asked around the ball of emotion choking his throat.

Rebecca turned her head, kissed the baby's cheek, and met his imploring gaze. "Sara. Sara Ann Marie."

She'd named her after his mother.

His knees shook. This wasn't what he'd expected. He'd thought he'd meet the kid, set up a monthly stipend to help with her needs, and maybe arrange for a visit now and then. But he never expected this onslaught of emotion. An immediate connection. A hunger to be an integral part of this child's growth and development. Her protector.

He sank to the floor, his back colliding with the wall. The girl's eyes grew wide, but he was too over-come to reassure her other than a faint smile that felt more like a grimace. She must have thought so too because she buried her head in her mother's shoulder and started to cry.

Ah, shit.

He didn't mean to scare her.

"Gus," Becky cried, hurrying to hand the child to the cook before rushing to his side and dropping to her knees. "Gus, what's wrong?"

She lifted a tentative finger to his face and brushed under his eye and that's when he realized he was crying. Embarrassed, he swiped at the moisture, closing his eyes until he gained some control. When he opened them, she'd sunk back on her heels and was staring at him while chewing on her bottom lip. She'd always done that when she was worried or upset. And many times, it had been his pleasure to kiss it all better.

He caught sight of her daughter—their daughter— staring at him while nibbling on a cookie the other woman had given her, and squirmed. It felt wrong to be thinking sexual thoughts about her mama.

He cleared his throat and shrugged uncomfortably. "I'm good now. Just had a bit of a dizzy spell, is all."

The toddler wriggled to get down, and after a nod from Rebecca, the cook let her go. She zeroed in on them, scooting across the floor in no time with her duck's waddle. As soon as she was near enough, she held out the mangled, half-eaten treat. "Cookie," she said, ordering him to take it.

Gus's stomach rebelled. He shook his head but refrained from the scary clown smiles this time. "No, thanks. You eat it."

Sara and Rebecca both looked at him as though he'd kicked their puppy. Ah, hell. He held out his hand. "How about we share?"

The baby's face lit up like a Christmas tree. She waddled the last few steps and plopped into his lap, pleased as punch. "Cookie," she said, lifting it to his startled lips.

He opened his mouth quick and tried hard not to think of the mushy taste. Oatmeal raisin, yum. Then he got a look at the delight shining on both his girls' faces and it was totally worth it.

Chapter Seventeen

CHANDLER COUNTY

Rebecca stared in consternation at her child sitting with such easy trust on the lap of someone who was essentially a stranger. She was caught between the urge to yank Sara away and climb up there with her. What would Gus do then?

He seemed endearingly baffled by the little girl chattering away in some incomprehensible language only she understood. His strong, capable hands cupped her little thighs, almost but not quite touching, and with that one small sign Becky's heart thawed. Even though he was terrified of children, his instinct was to protect.

"Do you want me to take her?" she asked, and suppressed a grin at his panicked look.

"Ah, yeah. If you don't mind?" he mumbled. "She's kind of... tiny. I'm scared I'll drop her."

Sara, dissatisfied now that she'd lost the stranger's attention, tapped him on the cheek with her sticky fingers. "Play," she demanded, her kewpie lips puckered in an annoyed frown.

Rebecca laughed. "She thinks you're her new playmate." She reached over and plucked the babe off his lap. "Leave the nice man alone before you scare him away, missy." She kissed her daughter on the nose. "Why don't you go and see if Aunty Jocelyn will show you her new puppy?"

That worked to turned the frown upside down. Sara's eyes lit up. "Puppy, Puppy," she chanted, scrambling off her mother's lap. With a combination crawling run that showed off her cute underpants with the frills across the bottom, she hurried into Jocelyn's waiting arms. "Puppy."

"Okay, chil', relax your little heart. I reckon we can go find Jelly Bean out back somewheres." She gave Gus the death-ray glare. "Don't you be messing with my girl now, you hear?"

Gus held up his hand. "No worries there, ma'am." He clambered to his feet and offered Becky a hand up. "I just have a few follow-up questions from the mur... other night. It won't take long."

Rebecca refused to analyze her disappointment. Of

course, if Gus said he was coming here to talk about Mr. Jorgenson, that's what he intended to do. It was foolish of her to harbor any dreams when it came to Augustus Grant; he was bound to let her down.

"Go ahead. I'll be fine with Detective Grant." She felt him stiffen by her side and had a little spurt of satisfaction. Two could play the cool-as-a-cucumber game. Jocelyn's corkscrew curls bounced as she marched across the kitchen and, with a last worried glance, left through the mudroom, Sara's chatter fading as they drifted away.

Then came the uncomfortable silence.

Needing something to do, Becky went to the sink and wet a clean towel. She returned to Gus's side and handed it over, pointing to his cookie-stained cheek. He swiped at it a couple of times, his gaze dark and watchful now they were alone.

"Good?" he asked.

Bowing to the inevitable, she shook her head and took the cloth, folding it carefully before she stepped closer and used his shoulder for balance to reach up and clean the area. His breath eased out in a soft whoosh that bathed her face and made her heart pound.

"Becky," he groaned.

She turned her head just that little bit and their lips met. Gus froze. Embarrassed she started to pull away, but he grabbed her waist and dragged her close. His mouth turned mobile, teasing and tempting, and oh-so-familiar.

God, she'd missed him.

She wound her arms around his neck, the cloth dropping unheeded to the ground, and gave herself up to the whirlwind of emotion flipping her body inside out. He'd always been a good kisser, but she'd forgotten how it affected her. How his muscular body felt against her softer curves. How fast she spun out of control in his arms. How good it all was.

The sound of a door closing nearby broke them apart.

It was a small solace to see Gus visibly shaken by what had just transpired. His eyes were glazed and his hand shook as he brushed it through his hair.

He rubbed his mouth. "Becky..."

Oh, no he wasn't.

There was no way she was going to stand there and take a gentle let down from him again. Been there, done that, had the engagement ring as a souvenir.

"Let it go, Gus." She bent to pick up the discarded cloth—and gain some much-needed breathing space. "It was just a kiss between old friends, nothing more." She threw the towel onto the table and turned to look at him, her hands gripping the tabletop at her back. "Why are you here, Gus? Is there news about...?"

He straightened his tie and cleared his throat. "Ah, no, not yet. We're working on it though. I have to ask... Can you tell me where you were on the night of April fifteenth, approximately between eight p.m. and midnight?"

Rebecca's blood ran cold. Should she lie? If he found out she'd gone to see Mr. Jorgenson the night he died, she would become a suspect. Oh, God, what could she say?

Feigning nonchalance, Becky pulled out a chair and sat, then immediately wished she hadn't. It put her at a disadvantage, one she could ill afford. "Why do you ask?" she hedged. "I thought Mr. Jorgenson's death was being treated as a suicide?"

Gus wandered the kitchen, picking up a spoon and setting it down, opening the oven to smell the roast, then carefully closing the door. It almost seemed like he was reluctant to lead her where she didn't want to go. But she knew better. The job would always come first with Augustus. It was who he was, and much as she hated it, she couldn't fault him for being a man of honor.

"I think that's what the killer wanted us to believe," he muttered around a mouthful of cookie. "But Mr. Jorgenson was definitely murdered. They found your prints in the room, Becky. On the furniture, and on the statue used to knock the victim to the floor before someone shot him in the head."

He looked up and met her gaze, his own dark and somber. "Now, can you please tell me where you were the night your boss was killed?"

Chapter Eighteen

CHANDLER COUNTY

J ocelyn smiled absently and handed the squeaky toy over to baby Sara playing in the sandbox Emmett done made her after she came to live on the estate with her momma. He was good, that man of hers. It weren't his fault that Mr. Jorgenson never saw the promise in him and kept him mucking out stalls like some stable boy when he should be the one trainin' them 'spensive race horses instead of that Mr. McMillon. Emmett said there was somethin' funny goin' on in them stables, and she believed it.

Somethin' that got poor Mr. Jorgenson shot dead.

She couldn't believe he was gone. What would happen to all of them now? Mrs. J. didn't care none about some stinkin' horses, all she cared about was appearances. Though a murdered husband tended to put a dent in that—muddied up the waters, it did.

Sara lifted a fistful of sand toward her mouth, but Jocelyn caught it just in time. "Tsk, child. Just 'cause they say you're going to eat a bushel and a peck before you grows up, doesn't mean you need to make it true."

Good-natured baby that she was, Sara gave up the sand and picked up a toy truck instead. One that looked a lot like Doc Baker's. "Now where did you get that, missy?"

"I bought it for her."

Startled, Jocelyn jumped at the deep voice of her husband coming from the path through the cottonwood trees leading to the sheds. She climbed up off her knees and hurried to his side, frowning at the tired look in his eyes. "Emmett Dawson Rose, you done scared ten years off my life. What're you doing sneakin' up on a person like that for?"

He smiled, the whites of his teeth flashing against his dark skin, and leaned down to give her a soft kiss. "Hello, wife. Isn't a man allowed to see his woman when he has an urge to anymore?"

She flushed, touched by the sincerity in his voice. "Of course. You surprised me, is all." She gazed up at this man who'd captured her heart with his strength and kindness. "I love you, baby."

His gaze warmed to molten chocolate and her insides melted into a gooey puddle. He'd always been able to turn her inside out with just a look—her lover.

He tugged her into his arms, her cheek coming to rest against his heart, his hands spanning her back. "Why do you have the baby?"

She closed her eyes and let the rumble of his voice vibrate down low, teasing her with the promise of intimacy.

Sighing, she lifted her head and smiled at the warmth in his expression. He would make a wonderful father. If he wasn't so darn stubborn. "Her momma is in the kitchen with Sara's daddy, the detective."

Emmett's arms stiffened, his gaze turning hard as he looked toward the main house, hidden behind the magnolia bushes. "Detective?"

Puzzled by his reaction, Jocelyn placed gentle fingers against his smooth jaw, bringing his attention back to her. "He's looking into Mr. Jorgenson's death. When are you going to tell me what this is about, husband? You've been acting strange for weeks now."

He hesitated, then turned his head to brush his lips against her palm, sending a shiver chasing down her spine. "It's nothing. Just the usual work hassles, don't worry so much."

She huffed out a breath. "It's my job to worry, I'm a woman, ain't I?"

He laughed, and she was relieved to see his tension ease. "You are definitely all woman, my love." He patted her on the butt. "You better get back to the baby, she must be hungry, she's attempting to empty the sandbox."

Jocelyn twisted in his grasp and sure enough, Sara's mouth was filled with sandy granules. "Oh, that chil'. She'll be pooping mud-pies for certain."

She started to pull away, but Emmett held her until she turned back to him. His gaze was somber and filled with regret. Before the dread could grab hold, he leaned down and kissed her with such warmth and emotion she forgot where they were standing.

"I love you," he murmured, then let her go, turning to walk with deliberate steps back toward the sheds.

Jocelyn watched until he was gone, fear weighing heavily on her chest that something worse than Mr. Jorgenson's murder was about to happen.

Chapter Nineteen

Chandler County

Augustus pretended a calm he didn't feel. When he'd received the report from the state crime lab that the prints on the statue matched one of the Jorgensons' employees, he hadn't expected it to be Rebecca. There had to be an explanation. He was just waiting to hear it.

"I don't think it's any of your business. Unless you plan to arrest me?" Becky said, her chin lifting in defiance.

Gus was tempted to pull out his handcuffs and see if that changed her tune. *Darn woman.*

He rounded the counter and sat beside her, reaching out to grasp her hand, aware of the little sizzle of electricity that passed through his body. "Becky, this is no time to be stubborn. You could be in serious trouble here." He gently squeezed her fingers. "I want to help, but you need to talk to me."

She tugged her hand free and sank back, arms crossed and green eyes crackling with hostility. "So, now you want to help. You're about two years too late, Augustus. I've had to sort things out on my own for quite a while now, and you know what I found?"

It was her turn to stand and pace the room. "I found people who care about me and my little girl. *Really care.*" She moved to the window by the back door and leaned against the wall. Her hand held the curtain aside, the sun dappling her upper body. "Sara is happy here. I'm happy here. Please, Gus, go away and leave us alone."

She said she was happy, but her body language told him something different. What was she hiding? It was almost as though she was protecting someone, but who? It was easy to blame him for not being there when she needed him, but then, she hadn't tried very hard either. If she had, he would've come. Or, at least, he'd like to think so. Truthfully, he hadn't deserved her back then. His sole focus had been geared on becoming a detective, and not just any gumshoe, the best.

He'd succeeded, but at what cost?

None of it mattered when compared to the simple joy of having your child sit in your lap and pat your cheek. His heart had overflowed in that moment.

Everything he thought he knew about his life plan changed in the blink of a set of baby blue eyes that looked at him, and accepted him, without judgement.

He'd been smitten.

All the more reason to keep her mama out of jail.

He tapped the table absently, trying to come up with the words to regain her trust.

"You always do that when you're thinking," she murmured, her voice filled with a poignant mix of tenderness and loss.

Remorse clawed up his throat, choking him with regret. "Becky..."

She dropped the curtain and faced him. "What? I'm not allowed to mention that you have an annoying habit of picking your teeth? And you never closed a cupboard door after you opened it, it used to drive me crazy." She sighed. "But, do you know what I remember most?"

He started to rise and she waved him down.

"No, stay there. This is hard enough as it is." Tears turned her eyes to emerald-washed stones. "I remember how it felt to wake up with you curled around me, warm and safe and secure. Loved, Augustus. You promised me a forever after, but that's not what transpired, is it? What happened to us?"

He stood and took her stiff body into his arms, the frantic beat of her heart a counter-point to his. God, he'd messed things up right royally. She was right, he had suggested marriage. Then he'd received that call to go to D.C., and he'd left her behind. At the time, he'd thought it would be short-term. He'd return home, maybe set up his own agency, and they could have the future they'd talked about. But the excitement of the chase, the thrill of solving crimes, had entered his bloodstream and he'd not so much forgotten, as placed Rebecca on a shelf in his heart. Something to be pulled down and dusted off occasionally, then returned for safe-keeping. She would wait until he was ready. After all, they loved each other.

How arrogant.

He didn't deserve a second chance, but that didn't stop him from praying she'd give him one anyway.

"How can I make it up to you, sweetheart?" He kissed her brow and brushed at the moisture dangling like stardust from her lashes. "It's always been you, Becky. You have to know that. I took a wrong turn, but I promise it won't happen again. I want a chance to get to know my daughter. I want to watch her grow and be there for her when she needs me. I want to scare her boyfriend when he comes to take her to prom night." A sobbing laugh escaped from Becky's lips. He smiled, choked up himself. "And I dream of walking her down the aisle and handing her over to someone who will love her as much as I love you."

Becky stilled, and gazed up at him with so much hope and doubt and disbelief, his heart cracked.

She pulled away, wrapping her arms tightly around her body as though to ward off a blow. "You almost had me there, Gus. Right up until the end anyway. What kind of mother would I be to allow you into Sara's life long enough for her to fall in love with you—she's already attaching herself to you—just to have you disappear when the next big case comes along?"

Anger grabbed hold. It wasn't all his fault, dammit. He'd been trying to make her proud. To *be somebody*. Not just the poor kid from town barely scraping a living.

"You know what?" he said. "You're probably right. It's too late to teach this old dog a new trick. I'm tired of jumping through hoops for you, Rebecca."

He grabbed his discarded hat and trench coat, and turned for the door. "The next move is yours."

Frustration drove him into the hall and out the front door before he realized he hadn't done what he'd come there to do in the first place.

Question his person of interest; Rebecca Hayes.

Chapter Twenty

By the time Gus arrived in Bourbonville his temper had disintegrated, leaving him with a bad taste in his mouth. He could have handled his conversation with Becky better. He'd rushed her, of course she'd backed away. There was more at stake than her giving him a second chance. She was a mother now, her priorities had to be with her daughter—with what she considered best for Sara's happiness.

And he had a case to solve. He needed to focus on Mr. Jorgenson's murder first, and then he could see about getting his life on track.

He passed a few more caravans heading to the fair grounds on his way to the sheriff's office. The carnival opened tomorrow night. He'd meant to ask Rebecca to the dance on Saturday, but things hadn't turned out so well between them. Maybe she already had plans with someone else. He rubbed his chest. Great, now he had indigestion.

Everywhere he looked, signs of the upcoming Kentucky Derby were apparent. Banners of blood-red roses twined with yellow and black ribbons hung from lamp post to lamp post, spanning the busy main street. Posters highlighting the upcoming events littered the windows of almost every business, from the barber shop to Rexall's Drug Store. It was an exciting time for the little town. For the length of the carnival and the Derby the following weekend, Bourbonville would swell to double its size. Every hotel, bed and breakfast, and rooming house between here and Lexington would be filled to capacity. It was good for the economy.

Not so good for solving a murder.

The sheriff's department was laboring to keep control over the crowds. Especially the rabble-rousing transients cutting loose with a few too many mint julips and bourbon cocktails. The jailhouse had a revolving door as one set of sobered customers were released to make room for their drunken counterparts. Tromley had already warned him to either help or get out of the way, he didn't have time to babysit. Friendly guy.

That's okay, Gus preferred to work on his own anyway. Then, any mistakes were his. Like the one he'd made this morning by letting personal issues interfere with an investigation.

He angled into a parking spot someone kindly freed up for him and tried to get out without hitting the side of the fancy Jaguar beside him. It took some finagling, but he did it and only closed his tie in the door of his car twice. A record.

He nodded to two women strolling down the sidewalk, one pushing a royal blue baby carriage, its springs creaking as the wheels rolled over the myriad of cracks in the cement. They smiled and giggled, carrying on down the walk with a flirtatious glance or two aimed his way. Gus grinned, warmed by their appraisal, and promptly tripped on the front steps of the sheriff's office.

"Excuse me."

Gus straightened and stared at the beautiful woman glowering down at him from the top stair. She wore a stylish white fitted dress, her long black hair coiled and covered by a matching pillbox hat. Her hands were covered by white kid-gloves and a powder-blue handbag dangling from her bent wrist completed the ensemble. She screamed class and Gus wondered what she was doing at the police station.

He stepped aside, giving her room to pass. "Pardon me, ma'am."

She slid a pair of cat-eye sunglasses onto the bridge of her dainty nose and glided down the stairs. She was even with him when he suddenly clued in to who she was.

Reflexively, Gus put his hand out to stop her descent. "Mrs. Jorgenson? Is that you, ma'am?"

She scowled, her lips pursed in disapproval. "Do you mind?"

He lifted his fingers off her sleeve. "Sorry about that."

She angled away from him, about to resume her journey down the stairs. Gus hurried to drop down a step and block her path.

"We haven't been formerly introduced," he said, holding out his hand. "Detective Grant, ma'am. I'm investigating your husband's murder."

She flinched. "I just heard. I... we all thought it was a suicide." She cupped her fingers and barely shook his hand before releasing it to dig in her purse for a handkerchief, dabbing delicately under each eye beneath the glasses. "It was such a shock."

Either she was genuinely upset, or she was one heck of an actress. Gus wasn't sure which.

"I'm sure it was. Can you tell me who might have wished your husband harm?" And when she shook her head, "Did he have any enemies that you were aware of?" He thought about the note he'd found in the deceased's desk. "Someone with a grudge, maybe?"

Mrs. Jorgenson took off her glasses and looked at him with somber brown eyes. "We're in one of the most competitive businesses in the world, Mr. Grant. Horse racing is a multi-million dollar industry. Of course, there are people who hold..." she clenched her gloved hand, "held a resentment of my husband's success. It's the nature of the beast. John was good at what he did—raising winning horses. I'm sure you know, this wasn't his first Kentucky Derby entry."

She looked toward Main Street. "The Derby affects more than just those in the trade. You might want to consider *that* during your investigation, Detective."

She was right, of course. He'd noted the economic growth of the town himself earlier. "Yes, ma'am, I surely will, thank you."

Tipping her head like a flower on the graceful stem of her neck, Mrs. Jorgenson took advantage of the space he'd given her and slid past, heading for the fancy Jaguar. Gus noticed the previously friendly people on the street now walked past without acknowledging one of their most esteemed citizens. Interesting.

She was about to step off the walk when he called out, "Pardon me, ma'am."

He waited, half expecting her to pretend she hadn't heard him. She wanted to, he could tell. Her shoulders tensed and she continued to the driver's side of the silver convertible before she looked at him.

"Yes, Mr. Grant?" she sighed her impatience.

Gus almost smiled. "Detective, ma'am. It's Detective Grant. Just one more question, if you don't mind."

"Certainly, *Detective*." She threw her purse into the car and opened the door. "What is it?"

"Mind telling me what you're doing at the sheriff's office, Mrs. Jorgenson?" Even if she and Tromley were having an affair, Gus couldn't see them bringing it into the public eye so soon after her husband's death. Which means this had to have been an official visit.

She got into the Jaguar—without coming near his car, he noticed—and slammed the door. Gus winced. He hated seeing such a fine piece of machinery treated roughly. The engine roared to life. She picked up a blue scarf from the seat beside her, wrapped it around her neck, and shifted into reverse before she answered.

"I fear someone is out to sabotage our chances at the Derby this year, Detective. They arrested my trainer, Mr. McMillon, on suspicion of horse drugging this morning." She backed out and swung into the driving lane, ignoring the annoyed honks from the cars behind her. "I'm going to Lexington to see a lawyer. Tell that pig-headed sheriff he'd better have a solid case by the time I return or he'll be sorry he's alive."

She roared off down the street in a cloud of venomous fury. Gus was reminded of the saying, *Hell hath no fury like a woman scorned.* He had a feeling Sheriff Tromley was going to be sorry he'd crossed swords with Trudy Jorgenson.

Chapter Twenty-One

Gus opened the door to a mob of angry citizens. All were vying for attention from the harried officers taking cover behind the long counter that cut the room in half. The previously quiet sanctuary he'd enjoyed at the sheriff's office was gone.

He didn't know what was going on, only that he wanted no part of it. He edged through the crowd and kept his head down, breathing a sigh of relief when he reached the door to the private office he'd been given to use without anyone calling his name.

"Hey, Detective, got a minute?" A lanky redhead raised a notepad in the air to get his attention.

Darn, so close.

"Depends on who's asking," he said when the guy had bulldozed his way over. He was young, barely out of school by the look of him. He wore black and white Oxfords teamed with a pale blue herringbone suit and polka-dot tie. Add that to the splattering of freckles bridging his nose and the copper hair cut military short under a rakishly tilted hat, and the kid was the brightest thing in the room. It wouldn't be long before they drew attention, already some of the nearby people were looking curious. Gus wasn't up to fielding a ton of unanswerable questions.

He ushered the man into the office and closed the door, leaning against it for a relieved second before striding across to his desk. "Have a seat, Mr....?"

"Randolph, sir. Leopold Randolph." The young man held out a hand and gave Gus a firm shake. "I work for the Chandlerville Chronicles. We're covering the story on the Jorgenson death and heard that it might now be a murder investigation?"

The kid was quick, Gus had to give him credit. The real question was who had told him the case changed? There were always loose lips in an inquiry. Someone who couldn't resist telling their family or friends, and then that person told someone, and so on, but he'd been hoping to keep it under his hat for at least another few days. Long enough to narrow his list of suspects anyway.

He sat back and gauged the reporter's interest. Intelligence shone in the blue-green gaze, and a desire to prove himself. Gus knew that feeling all too well. Mr. Randolph wasn't going to be easily put off with a fabricated story.

Gus decided to go on the offensive. "Mind telling me who told you this is a murder?"

Leopold smiled. "You know I can't divulge a source, Detective. Let's just say it's someone interested in getting to the bottom of this story and leave it at that." He leaned forward. "Does that mean you *are* searching for a killer?" His eyes lit up, probably picturing his name under the day's headline, the rapscallion.

"Tell you what, you share anything you know and I'll guarantee you get the exclusive when the case breaks. Deal?" It was a calculated risk—and Tromley wouldn't like it—but reporters were known for their ferreting skills. Some cops considered them little more than rats—not Gus. As long as the suspect was apprehended, he didn't care who helped with the investigation.

Leopold tapped long, lean fingers on the desk. Gus could practically see him weighing the pros and cons, and he saw when the pros won. The kid would never make a poker player.

"Okay, but you better not be pulling my leg." He eyed Gus up just short of uncomfortable, then nodded as though reaching a decision. "I received a message this morning that something big was about to go down, and if I wanted to know who killed John Jorgenson I should get my patootie down to the Bourbonville Sheriff's Department, pronto."

So, his source was a woman then. No self-respecting guy was going to tell another man to move his *patootie*. Sheesh.

"Is that why you were standing out there with that mob?" Gus lifted his chin toward the door.

Randolph nodded. "Yes, sir. Rumor has it the Jorgensons' trainer was just brought in for questioning. Those people are his family and friends. They're demanding to know what's going on."

Good question. Gus wanted to know the same thing. The sheriff was supposed to be collaborating with him on this case, not trying to run the show himself.

"What can you tell me about the trainer?" He'd been away from these parts for a long time. After school and the breakup of his marriage, he hadn't been able to wipe the dust of Bourbonville off his shoes fast enough. Then he'd been called to Lexington on the Keller murder and had fallen in love with a young woman's emerald green eyes and captivating smile. His time with Becky was like breathing clean mountain air after years of smog—invigorating and addicting. Which made it all the more inconceivable that he'd let her get away. If he were honest with himself, he'd have to admit his feelings for her had scared him. After the debacle of his marriage to Marnie, he'd been gun-shy. He'd mistrusted his instincts. Never again. That mistake had cost him the love of his life and a daughter. And the worst of it was, he wasn't sure he could ever make it up to them.

"Steve McMillon has been around the racing circuit for most of his life. His ol' man was a famous trainer. Steve did pretty good as a jockey until he took a bad spill. He even went up against *The Shoe* a couple of times, and almost won. That's why this race is such a big deal. It's the first time the two of them will be— would have been," he corrected, "going head-to-head, so to speak, since the accident."

"The Shoe?" Gus asked, his brow crinkling.

Leopold sat up, animated. "Bill Shoemaker, the jockey. You must have heard of him. He's set to make the record in victories this year. The man's a legend."

"So, this is an important race then?" Gus knew nothing about Thoroughbred racing. Embarrassing, since he was a born and bred Kentuckian, but there you go.

Leopold's rusty red eyebrows climbed into his hair-line. "You're kidding, right? The Kentucky Derby, held at Churchill Downs, is the first of three races comprising The Triple Crown, the greatest accom-

plishment in Thoroughbred racing. The Derby is one
and a quarter miles long. Next is the Preakness, held at
the Pimlico Race Course in Baltimore, Maryland. It's a
mile and three-sixteenths. Then, there's the grand-
daddy of them all, the Belmont Stakes, held in New
York. It's the longest at a mile and a half. There's only
ever been eight horses to win the title, but this year
Native Dancer—The Gray Ghost—has a good chance
of taking it. This would be his twelfth win, he's
undefeated.

"But then you have The Shoe riding Invigorator,
and Mr. McMillon with his horse, Forever Humble,
and this is lining up to be a race for the history books.
Which is why I don't see Mr. McMillon doing what
they accused him of, besides, he and the second Mrs.
Jorgenson had a thing awhile ago, so I think his loyalty
will be with her."

Gus tried to take in all the information that had
just been dumped in his lap. It seemed like Mrs.
Jorgenson and this McMillon guy were at the center of
everything. Which meant he needed to interview the
trainer again.

And find out where Rebecca fit into all of this
before she was the next one Tromley decided to arrest.

Chapter Twenty-Two

CHANDLER  COUNTY

Rebecca sighed and straightened her spine, stopping to rub the ache in her lower back. Mrs. Jorgenson's after-party dress was nearing completion. All she had left to add was the Venetian lace for the sweetheart neckline, along with ruffled straps and short sleeves open to show off the shoulder. The embroidered top in a pretty, floral inspired pattern, flowed into a sheer bottom with two layers of feminine ruffles.

She loved everything about this dress. From the moment she'd come across the pattern at the fabric shop, Becky had dreamed of wearing it to the dance on carnival night. She'd been tempted to keep the pattern and make the gown for herself, but she could never afford the material a dress like this demanded. The smart thing would have been to choose another outfit for Mrs. J and leave that one in the store, but, like a diabetic craving a piece of sweet candy, she couldn't leave it alone.

The lace was exquisite. A pale beige with the faintest hint of a blush, it fell in soft folds to just below the knees at a slight angle and would swirl with the barest of movements. It was a dress meant to catch a man's attention. And in her heart of hearts, she wanted Augustus to see her wearing it.

There, she'd said it, if only to herself.

Maybe if he was reminded of the young woman he'd fallen in love with, he could grow to care for her again. She thought of his words from the other day and the ready tears trembled on her lashes. If only she could trust him.

"Oh, my lord, that's plum beautiful." Jocelyn breezed into the sunroom, a duster in one hand and a watering can in the other. "Is that for the dance?" she said, her voice hushed as she stared in awe at the gown draped over a headless mannequin.

Becky smiled and struggled to her feet, groaning a little at the stiffness in her knees. She'd overdone it, but hadn't wanted to stop when the lace stitching was going together so well. She fingered the cap sleeve. "It's something, isn't it?"

"Girlfriend, that dress was made for you," Jocelyn said, and set her cleaning supplies down before joining her. "You're going to be the talk of the town in that gown."

"It's not for me," Becky said, trying to control the wistful longing curling like smoke through her chest.

Jocelyn touched her arm. "Oh, honey. I'm sorry."

Becky shrugged. "Don't be. I'm sure Mrs. J will look wonderful. She can do it better justice than me, anyway."

"Here now, I don't want to hear that kind of talk," Jocelyn exclaimed. "You're sweet and kind, and the most beautiful gal in Bourbonville. Ask anyone."

Becky gave her friend a quick hug, then turned away to gather her composure. "Where's Sara?" Immediately after saying it, she twisted back, embarrassed with the accusing tone in her voice. "Gah, what's wrong with me? I'm sorry, Jocelyn." She grabbed hold of her friend's work-roughened hands and gave them a squeeze. "I'd never be able to manage without you. I'm a complete jerk, ignore me."

Jocelyn's teeth shone white against her dark skin. "Don't you worry about that little one. Emmett and me, we won't let anything happen to her while we have her. She's down for a nap, he's home for lunch so he said he'd watch her while I gets a little extra cleaning done for the missus."

"Truly, I can't thank you enough," Becky said, moving to water the assortment of plants decorating the picture window sills while Jocelyn swept up the dust. "Are you and Emmett planning to go to the dance tomorrow night?"

Jocelyn nodded, her expression dreamy. "My man dances like Fred Astaire." She held the duster in her arms and twirled around the room humming. "You should come. Even without that party dress, you'll be a hit."

Becky was tempted, there was no denying that. It had been a long time since she'd gone out on the town —before she'd found herself pregnant. It would be nice to let her hair down for awhile. Except, she had no date and no one to watch her daughter.

She sighed. "I can't. You guys go and have a good time, you deserve it."

Jocelyn quit dancing and dropped the dust-mop on the floor, then placed her hands on her hips and glared across the space dividing them. "Why cain't ya? If you're worried about the baby, Miss Sadie has offered more than once to take her. And since she done did raise five of her own, I'm sure one more for a night won't hurt.

"As to a date, what about that there detective daddy of yours? He looks like he could hold his own on the dance floor."

He never asked me.

She gave a dis-jointed laugh. "Gus is too busy

chasing bad guys to take me out. Besides, I'm not sure I'd say yes anyway."

Jocelyn let her hands fall, and her expression turned mischievous. "I say, let's give that man something to regret." She hurried across and cradled Becky's hands against her generous bosom. "C'mon, honey. It'll be fun. I bet Ernest would take you. He's been wanting to ask you out for months now."

It's true, she'd sensed the manservant's interest. He was an attractive man, in a butlerish sort of way, but her heart was taken. She hadn't been out with anyone since Augustus. Maybe Jocelyn was right. A night on the town *would* be fun, and if Gus heard about it maybe it would prod him into action. He'd talked about loving her and Sara, but so far she hadn't seen anything to prove she'd made the wrong decision in turning him away.

She smiled into her friend's warm brown eyes. "Okay, you've talked me into it. But what am I going to wear? All my clothes are made for function, not frivolity."

A sly grin crossed Jocelyn's lips. "That's the easy part. Mrs. J's dress, of course."

Becky's eyes widened. She shook her head, all the while sneaking glances at the gorgeous gown draped over the mannequin, tempting her to do something totally crazy. Something that could cost her job.

"No," she murmured. "It would be wrong. What if Mrs. Jorgenson found out? It probably won't fit anyway. Mrs. J is so fine-boned."

"If you mean skinny, she is that alright." Jocelyn spanned her hands around Becky's waist. "But, so are you. It'll fit, I know it will. Mrs. J won't mind, she never attends the carnival. It's not her thing. And besides, she's got a closet full of fancy clothes. She probably won't even notice."

Oh, man, she couldn't believe she was going to do this, but the excitement had her in its grip now. She was tired of doing the safe and dull lifestyle—it was time to show Bourbonville what Rebecca Hayes was made of.

"Okay, let's do this." She placed a trembling hand to her belly to still the butterflies and smiled nervously as Jocelyn let out a victory whoop and picked up her dust-mop to continue dancing in celebration.

Why did she feel like she'd just made a monumental mistake?

Chapter Twenty-Three

CHANDLER COUNTY

Gus ushered Leopold Randolph out the door a short time later and was happy to see the foyer had been cleared.

Sheriff Tromley stood at the counter and looked up from his perusal of some documents. "Talking to reporters now, Grant? How many state secrets did you spill?"

Gus ignored his snide remarks to wander over and tip his head sideways to see what the other man was reading. "This the Jorgenson trainer's arrest sheet?"

Tromley slapped the file closed, his thick brows meeting above the bridge of his nose. "Suppose the kid told you that?"

Gus shrugged. Let Stan think what he liked. There was no benefit in telling the sheriff about his run-in with Trudy Jorgenson. But, he was curious about something.

"He mentioned Mrs. Jorgenson and Mr. McMillon were an item not long ago. You know anything about that, Stan?"

Instead of answering, the sheriff pushed away from the counter and carried the overflowing file to the lineup of cabinets decorating the back wall. He stood in front of one, started to open it, then suddenly slammed his fist against the drawer, startling Gus when it crashed closed.

He threw the file on top of the cabinet, then turned and glared across the distance. "Watch your mouth, Grant. Trudy—Mrs. Jorgenson—isn't that kind of a woman. There's a bunch who are cynical about her reasons for marrying a man double her age, but I've known her since she was a kid. She loved her husband. It's bullcrap if anyone says anything different."

That may be true, but Gus had a feeling it hadn't stopped Stan Tromley from falling head-over-heels for the beautiful brunette.

"Any idea what she plans to do with that big ol' horse ranch now her husband is gone?" Gus asked, tapping his fingers on the counter in a deliberate rat-a-tat-tat that had the sheriff scowling. "I don't imagine it would be easy for a woman to run a Thoroughbred operation successfully."

"What the hell does that mean?" Stanley grimaced and flexed reddened knuckles. "No reason Trudy couldn't run that ranch just as good, or even better than Jorgenson ever did. He wasn't nothing like his daddy anyway. Now that man had horse sense. John was just playing at it—he had no real respect for the industry."

Hmm, it was sounding increasingly like all was not what it seemed on the Jorgenson estate. "Mind if I go back and have a chat with McMillon?" He had some questions for the trainer, namely what he might know about that handwritten note he'd found in the Jorgensons' study.

Do what I told you to do, or the truth will destroy you.

Tromley hesitated, then shrugged. "I guess I can't prevent ya. Just make sure you ask if he wants a lawyer first. He turned me down earlier, but that didn't stop Trudy from haring on out of here to hire him one anyway."

Gus knew it would only cause a fight to remind the sheriff he was a detective and was aware of proper protocol, so he just nodded. "I'll keep it short. Mind telling me exactly what the charges are?"

Stan tugged an overburdened key ring from his sagging tan trouser pocket and turned toward the door to the cells. "Officially, the illegal doping of horses. We have Spencer Drayton, Sr. with the Thoroughbred

Racing Protective Bureau breathing down our necks so we better keep it legit."

Was there another way?

Gus mused on the sheriff's strange choice of words as he followed him into the clean, but dank room. Dayton was a decorated member of the F.B.I. Gus remembered hearing he'd been recommended by the Hoover administration to head up a new investigative team.

There was a corridor down the middle of the room with three cells lining each side. The cement floor was cracked and carried dark stains that he side-stepped and tried not to think about what had caused them. His nose crinkled. The scent of unwashed bodies combined with alcohol and excrement from the five gallon pails set up for use in each stall was over-whelming in the tight space.

Tromley noticed his instinctual reaction and grinned. "What's the matter, Detective? Were you expecting *The Ritz*?"

"Hah, ha. You're a barrel of laughs, Sheriff," Gus muttered, breathing through his mouth.

All but one of the cells were occupied, the men in them sullen and rough around the edges. But then, a few days in this place would do that to him, too.

"Get up, McMillon," Tromley rattled the cell door before jamming a key in the lock and giving it a twist.

The door opened with only a slight protest, revealing a bulky man lying on a cot against the far wall.

He lifted his head and looked at them over his shoulder, then slowly rolled into a sitting position. He rubbed a hand over a jaw covered in bristles, his dark hair standing up on one side, and glared at them from baggy reddened eyes. "I already told you, I got nothin' to say."

Stan leaned against the bars and stuck his thumbs in the waistband of his pants. "Fine with me. You can stay here until your parole hearing. Makes no difference one way or the other."

McMillon slid a suspicious glance Gus's way. "What's he want?"

He surged to his feet, surprising Gus with his short stature until he remembered the man had once been a jockey.

"You can just leave. I already told Ms. Jorgenson I cain't afford no pencil pusher."

Gus stepped forward, careful not to make any sudden moves. The man seemed edgy enough. "No need for a lawyer, sir." He ignored the sheriff's, "Grant", and held out a hand. "We met at the ranch? I was wondering if I could ask you a few questions about the Jorgenson murder."

McMillon's eyes widened. "I don't know nothin' about no murder." He turned to Tromley. "What's he talking about, Stan? You're not thinking I had some-thing to do with Mr. Jorgenson's death, are you?"

The sheriff straightened. "Did you?" He took a menacing step forward. "If you did anything to hurt Trudy, I'll... I'll..."

Gus hurried to step between the two combatants. "Sheriff, I'd appreciate it if you'd let me speak to Mr. McMillon on my own for a few minutes." He traded glares with the lawman until Stan finally backed down.

He turned and walked out, swinging the bars closed behind him. "Whatever. Don't blame me if this lowlife tries to slit your throat." He locked the door and walked away, his back rigid.

Gus waited until the outer door opened and closed and McMillon's cellmates went back to staring at the walls before he tried again.

"I hear you were quite the jockey, Mr. McMillon. Some say one of the best." Gus looked around the bare-bones cell. "Your family and friends are worried about you. They drove the sheriff plum crazy this morning. Why don't you tell me what happened and I'll see if I can't get you back home with them?"

McMillon snorted. "Home. What home? By the time the dust settles on this mess I'll be jobless. I tried to...." He glanced at the other men occupying the jail and abruptly cut off whatever he'd been about to say.

"It doesn't matter anyway. By the time I make bail the damage will be done."

Gus nodded like he knew what the other man was talking about. He decided to take different tack. "Mind telling me how long you worked for the Jorgensons, Mr. McMillon? Were they good to their employees?"

The trainer rubbed a hand over his head, mussing his hair even more. "It's Steve. Mr. McMillon was my dad." He shuffled back to the cot and sank down with a tired sigh. "I've been on Balmoral's payroll—the estate —ever since Jorgenson bought Forever Humble two years ago." A light of pride turned his non-descript eyes the color of a spring leaf. "That colt was all attitude. He wouldn't let anyone come near without taking a bite outta them first. They called me in because I had a name for handling the difficult ones. Didn't take long before I knew Humble was special. We ran him in a few races, trying to get a feel for his pacing, whether he liked a fast track or a muddy one. It didn't matter. Nothing slowed that horse down."

He slapped the mattress beside him as though urging the pony on. "We were sitting pretty for the Derby, and with Native Dancer taking all the heat as the favorite, Jorgenson stood to make a pile of cash too. That's why it made no damn sense to do what they wanted me to do. I told them to forget it, but..."

Gus's pulse did a drum solo in his chest. He was close, he could feel it.

"Who's they, Mr.... Steve?" He shoved suddenly sweaty hands into his pant pockets before he grabbed the other man and shook the information out of him. "And what did they want you to do?"

Steve bowed his head and Gus had to lean forward to hear his words. "*They* are the loan sharks Trudy got herself mixed up with. Either I dope Humble to ensure a win, or they were going to tell her husband about our affair."

Chapter Twenty-Four

CHANDLER  COUNTY

Rebecca ambled through the park, her arm tucked into the crook of Ernest's elbow, Emmett and Jocelyn following close behind. There was so much to see, from tents filled with baked goods and handcrafts, to games of fortune. Something for everyone, and it appeared half the county was here to take advantage of the lovely spring evening. In the center of the field the Ferris wheel turned slowly against the skyline, stopping every now and then to the delighted shouts of those caught at the top, while the carnival scents of cotton candy, popcorn, hot dogs, and elephant ears added to the overall excitement riding the crowd. Music from the fair grounds along with fairy lights strung up in the trees and framing the tents created an otherworldly feel to the normally vacant field.

"Ooh, where should we go first?" Jocelyn exclaimed. "I wish the carnival were here year-round."

"Then, I really would be broke," Emmett grumbled good-naturedly.

Becky glanced back to smile at her friends. "I'm glad you talked me into coming." She squeezed Ernest's arm. "Thank you for agreeing to be my date on such short notice."

He looked very dapper tonight in a dark blue dress-coat paired with pleated tan trousers. A fedora tipped low on his forehead completed the ensemble. He nodded, his expression benign. "I'm honored to be here, Miss Rebecca."

"Oh, please, all my friends call me Becky," she teased, feeding off the buoyancy of the crowd.

"Well, Miss Becky, might I say you look lovely this evening." His dark eyes roved over her *borrowed* dress, lingering on the sweetheart neckline.

Uncomfortable, Rebecca straightened the lace shawl around her shoulders, pulling it forward to cover her throat. She glanced up and caught an indefinable *something* in his expression before it disappeared, replaced by a slight smile. She was jerked out of the awkward moment by Jocelyn's delighted squeal.

"Look," she cried. "The shooting gallery. You have to try, Emmett. Sara would love one of those teddy bears. Please, baby."

Emmett gazed at his wife and a big grin split his lips. "You're sure it's for the chil' now, is it?"

"Emmett Dawson Rose, what do you take me for?" Jocelyn huffed, her dusky face shining under the glow of the lights.

She tugged him toward the crowd gathered at the front of a tent with two orange wheels slowly twirling, each with a variety of numbered cards tacked into the wood. A line of ducks popped up randomly in the front row, tempting a competitor to waste his turn with an easy mark. The back wall and ceiling were filled with an assortment of stuffed bears, dogs, giraffes, even a pink elephant. Men lined up in groups of three, a rifle in hand and took aim, some coming away with prizes, and others with lighter pockets.

The easy camaraderie of the night had been broken by Ernest's appraisal. Rebecca cast an anxious glance at Jocelyn disappearing into the throng before turning to her date with a determined smile.

"We should probably catch up, we don't want to lose them in the crowd." She tried to unobtrusively break free of his suddenly tight grip on her arm. "Ernest, you're hurting me."

He'd been staring at something over her shoulder and when she spoke he startled, as though just remembering she was there. "How about a ride on the Ferris wheel?"

"No, I..." Before she could finish, he practically yanked her through the bystanders, jostling a few along the way.

"Hey, watch it," a teenager in a black leather coat and greased back hair growled.

"Shut yer trap, before I shut it for you," Ernest snapped, his eyes razor sharp in the lengthening shadows.

Something was drastically wrong. The man she knew as a stalwart, loyal servant of the Jorgensons had morphed into a monster. Becky's heart stuttered. Panicking, she twisted her wrist, desperate to escape his hold, to no avail.

"What are you doing? Let me go before I scream for help." Between the enormous crowd and the cacophony created by the piped-in music playing from every stall, barely anyone had noticed her plight.

"Keep quiet, or that kid of yours will be an orphan," he snarled, his gaze sliding over her shoulder again.

Becky gasped, fear turning her overheated skin to ice. She glanced back and caught a glimpse of the sheriff's hat trailing them through the crowd. Hope flared, then crashed when she realized Ernest was aware of the lawman.

And she'd just become a hostage.

Chapter Twenty-Five

CHANDLER  COUNTY

Gus didn't have time to wander the fairgrounds helping the sheriff keep the peace, but when asked, he hadn't been able to refuse. Between concern for his *friend*, Trudy Jorgenson, and his duty to the town, Stan Tromley was feeling the stress. And besides, Gus owed Bourbonville a show of loyalty. This town had stood behind him when his own family had not. They'd ensured a poor kid from the wrong side of the tracks had the education needed to prove to Gus's dad he wasn't the useless piece of crap he'd been labeled.

He nodded to a few familiar faces, broke up a pair of squabbling teens, and tried not to think about the last time he'd attended this fair. Impossible when everything around him carried poignant memories.

Becky's smile as she teased him with cotton candy, her laughter when he turned green on the tilt-a-whirl, and the heady taste of her kisses atop the Ferris wheel. They'd consummated their love that night and he'd known then she was his soulmate. His previous marriage to Marnie had been a mistake. Young kids with too many pheromones. It hadn't taken long to realize they were totally unsuited out of the bedroom. Rebecca was different. She'd challenged him on every level. Life with her would never be boring.

If only he could convince her to give him another chance.

A young couple sat on a plaid-striped blanket under a willow tree near the concession booths. A wicker picnic hamper lay open, but forgotten, beside them. They were in their own little world, barely taking note of their surroundings. Gus envied them.

A commotion near the Ferris wheel dragged his attention away. Sighing, he turned toward the fracas, expecting to see more teens testing their oats. Instead, his gaze connected with Rebecca's frightened eyes as she was yanked through the crowd by a man in a fedora.

Shock rocked his body. He hadn't expected to see her tonight, and definitely not this way. She'd acted as though she was... in danger.

His brain caught up to what he'd just seen and he

hurried forward, bouncing on his toes to keep the dark hat in view over the swirling crowd. Who was she with? He hadn't been able to get much of a glimpse other than a fleeting impression of dark hair and a stern jaw. All manner of horrible scenarios floated through his mind, undoubtedly a legacy of his job. Maybe it was nothing more than a disgruntled date calling an end to the night. Gus wasn't any happier thinking about Becky out with another man, but it was better than the alternative.

He punched through a gap in the crowd and stumbled to a halt. They'd disappeared. He spun right, then to the left, his breathing erratic as he searched faces in the encroaching darkness.

Where were they?

"Grant, you see them?"

The sheriff's voice coming from behind swung him around. He was shocked to see Tromley stalking toward him with his gun drawn. The crowd took one look at the weapon and the grim man carrying it, and faded away.

Gus kept his arms out from his sides, just in case. "Mind telling me what's going on, Sheriff?"

Instead of answering, Tromley waved him toward the now deserted willow tree, the hamper tipped on its side and the blanket scrunched from many feet.

He hesitated, concern overriding common sense.

"Put the gun down, Stanley. I don't have time for your theatrics. Someone has taken Rebecca Hayes. I need your help."

Tromley ordered a couple of officers standing behind him to fan out, then he holstered his weapon. "I'm aware of Miss Hayes dilemma, Detective. What do you think we're here for?" He stepped nearer. "If it were just to maintain the crowd, my men know their jobs. We had a tip that our murder suspect would be here tonight. I wasn't expecting the butler, but it makes sense when you think about it."

Gus shook his head, feeling as though he were under water and hearing everything through a vacuum. "You're telling me you used Rebecca," he shouted, "to lure a murderer to a fair filled with innocent lives? Are you loco?"

The sheriff glared. "Keep your damn voice down. The idea is to sneak up on him, not broadcast that we're here."

Gus wiped a trembling hand over his mouth. "What did you mean, it makes sense?"

Tromley glanced around, then leaned in as though he were imparting a state secret. "After you told us what McMillon said, I did a little digging. Seems our good butler, Ernest, has some serious mob connections. None of it would have come to light without you finding out about the horse doping." He frowned and spit off to the side. "Trudy's been gambling on all those so-called shopping trips she likes to take in Lexington. When Jorgenson found out, he threatened to cut her off. Somehow, she managed to borrow against the ranch's livestock, which is when Ernest showed up. She *hired* him as an apology to John. In reality, he was ordered there to keep an eye on the mob's investment."

Suddenly, the note made sense.

Do what I told you to do, or the truth will destroy you

It must have been Ernest warning Mrs. Jorgenson to toe the line, or else. Gus remembered reading something about the growing problem in the racing industry. Trainers fed the animals sometimes lethal cocktails in a bid to have the horses run even if they had swollen joints or bleeding lungs. Anything for the win.

None of which explained why Rebecca was here with a killer.

"If anything happens to Becky..." he growled.

"Nothing will happen," Stan said. "We have the park surrounded and my men are searching even as we speak. Don't worry, your girlfriend will be fine."

If he weren't so worried, Gus would wipe that sarcastic smile off the jerk's face, sheriff or no sheriff. But right now, all he wanted was to wrap his arms around his woman and hold on tight.

"What's our next move?" he asked, pushing past the taller man.

"We're at the carnival, let's have a little fun." Tromley answered.

Chapter Twenty-Six

CHANDLER  COUNTY

Rebecca couldn't believe this was happening. Maybe it was punishment for wearing a dress that didn't belong to her. Now, she was getting hysterical. Who could blame her though? The worst of it was, she had a sick feeling this had something to do with Mr. Jorgenson's death. And if that were true...

Ernest kept his head down and a vise grip on her wrist as he tugged them deeper into the fair grounds. Becky had stopped trying to let people know she needed help after he'd shown her the gun tucked under his jacket. She couldn't bear to be the cause of anyone getting injured. Nor did she wish to take a chance on him living up to his threat to kill her.

Sara needed her mother.

She sneaked a glance under her arm, but everything was a blur thanks to the tears pouring down her face. She thought she'd caught a glimpse of Gus, but when moments passed without a rescue, she had to assume she was mistaken. Wishful thinking and a whole lot of praying.

"Ernest, please," she gasped. "If you have a shred of decency..."

He veered suddenly to the left, almost knocking an elderly woman to the ground. She raised her cane and shook it, glaring at them. "Watch where you're going, you hooligans."

If the situation weren't so dire, Becky would have laughed. If there was one thing she'd never had a chance to be, it was a troublemaker. She'd been too busy being the perfect daughter in a house filled with over-achievers.

"You should have minded your own business," Ernest muttered, ducking around the side of a tent filled with a penned assortment of farm animals, some sporting long blue ribbons.

Rebecca gaped. "Are you crazy? You're the one who kidnapped me."

He dropped her arm to check his weapon and peek around the edge of the canvas.

"You're not going to get away with this, you know."

He glared over his shoulder. She shivered and rubbed her reddened wrist.

"How much did Jorgenson tell you?" He turned and his lips quirked. "Mind you, I can see why he liked to spend time with such a pretty little thing." He reached out to touch her face and Becky jumped back, revulsion churning in her stomach.

"Don't touch me," she spat. "You're a... a monster." Laughter erupted nearby, a jarring contrast to the dangerous man she was facing. "What did you hope to achieve?"

"Well, that's the funny part," he murmured. "Until I saw the sheriff and his merry men I thought this was going to be a pleasant night with a beautiful woman. A little dancing, maybe some snuggling." The intensity in his gaze did little to warm her. "But now I get it." The heat gave way, turning his eyes a flinty gray. "This was all a setup. You thought you could lure me down here and get me to confess to the old man's death within earshot of the detective, didn't you?"

He grabbed her arm and shook her. Hard. "Didn't you?"

"No," she cried. "I don't know what you're talking about. Please, just let me go." Rebecca twisted, trying with all her might to break free of his hold.

"You heard the lady." A voice snapped from behind Ernest. "You're completely surrounded. If you know what's good for you, set that weapon down real slow like and step away from Rebecca."

Gus.

Time slowed. Ernest's stare went from shocked to menacing just before he yanked her into his arms and held the pistol to her temple.

Becky gasped, the cold metal burning a hole where it pressed against her flesh. He forced her head back at an awkward angle against his shoulder, the other arm wrapped under her breast, squeezing her ribs as though he were a boa constrictor and she was his quarry. She prayed she'd pass out before he shot her. Memories of how poor Mr. Jorgenson had died flashed like a newsreel before her panic-stricken eyes.

Please, God, don't let my baby lose her momma like this.

"It's over, Ernest. I told Stan everything."

His body jolted on hearing Mrs. Jorgenson's words. He swung them toward the sound, the crowd around them flashing by at a dizzying speed.

"You dumb bitch," he snarled, the gun gouging Becky's head. "You couldn't do what you were told. None of this needed to happen if you had just listened."

He was losing control of the situation and knew it. Becky pinned all her faith on Augustus. She could feel him waiting, watching. Ready to dive in and be the hero.

Her hero.

"Listening to you is what got me into this mess to begin with," Trudy said. "If I'd gone to John, asked for help, my husband would still be alive."

"I's heard him trying to force Mrs. J to make McMillon give them drugs to the horses, jus' like I told you, Sheriff." Emmett's deep voice came from the shadows.

"I have your statement, Emmett. You've been a big help closing this ring down. We couldn't have done it without you," the sheriff said.

"There's more," Emmett moved forward, his face grim as he took in the gun against Becky's head. He turned to Gus.

"That's enough, *boy*," the sheriff growled.

"No, sir, it's not." Emmett hesitated, his gaze imploring Jocelyn to understand. "I had no choice. They said they'd kill you if I didn't do what they wanted."

Jocelyn stood on the fringes of the crowd, her expression enough to break Becky's heart.

"Lord, Emmett, what did you do?"

"I did what I was told," he snarled, his tone venomous as he pointed at Ernest, who squeezed Becky's ribs plumb through to her backbone. "The sheriff and him... they're in it together. The sheriff, he done hate Mr. Jorgenson. Mrs. J was scared when Mr. J found out about her gambling addiction, he'd divorce her. Make her a laughing stock. The sheriff wasn't having none of it. He came up with a plan to make it look like Mr. J was druggin' his horses and then he was going' to threaten to arrest him."

Ernest turned the barrel of the gun away from Becky and pointed it at Emmett. "Shut the hell up. I told the sheriff you weren't to be trusted."

Again, Emmett brought everyone's attention back to Ernest, his eyes flashing. "But, Mrs. J already went to *him*. He gave her the money she'd taken from the estate, but it came at a price. He needed a place to funnel the mob's dirty money, so Tromley helped him blackmail Mr. J into using his stables to put perfectly good racehorses out to stud. Lots of money changing hands and no one's the wiser."

A shot rang out and Jocelyn screamed. Emmett got a stunned look on his face. He glanced down at his chest and frowned at the burgeoning red stain.

"He wrecked my good Sunday-go-to-meeting shirt," he said as Jocelyn hurried to his side.

Becky blinked away her tears, desperate to see if he was going to be alright as a crowd of police circled the area. Two men grabbed Sheriff Tromley and relieved him of his weapon, and two more stepped forward, guns raised toward Ernest, shouting for him to drop his weapon.

All the different voices coming at them like stabs

from the dark were causing Ernest's confidence to bleed out. His arm had loosened and just as he let the gun lower Gus was there, yanking her to the safety of his arms as what seemed like an army of men swarmed the hapless manservant.

GUS WRAPPED BECKY IN HIS WARM JACKET AND led her away from the crowd of curious onlookers. The sheriff's men could handle the arrests. As long as Rebecca was safe, he didn't give a damn about protocol.

That was too close.

When he'd seen the gun pressed against her porcelain skin, he'd been as near as he'd ever been to killing a man in cold blood.

Now that it was over she was sobbing and his limbs felt like wet noodles. They needed a place to talk where no one could bother them.

He glanced around and spotted what he was looking for. "Hold on, baby. I've got you."

It took some persuasion and a flash of his badge, but soon they were on the Ferris wheel, headed to the top of the world. He kept an arm wrapped protectively around her and gazed down at the spot where he'd almost lost his reason for living. His stomach rolled picturing that gun pointed at her head and his sheer helplessness to stop it from happening. No amount of training could have prepared him for the sheer terror he'd felt in those moments.

He'd do what he could to get Rebecca's friend's sentence lowered. The man had been unbelievably brave to step forward the way that he had. They might never have learned the full story without him.

He kissed Becky's brow and contemplated the new facts, surprised he hadn't connected the dots faster. It all seemed so obvious to him now. If Tromley loved his Trudy half as much as Gus loved Rebecca, no wonder he'd fought to keep her name clean. He'd been trying to protect her secret.

Meanwhile, Ernest had his own gameplay, forcing Mr. Jorgenson to funnel mob money and it better explained the mysterious note—*Do what I told you to do, or the truth will destroy you.*

So many lives ruined for the sake of gambling. If only Trudy would have confessed to her husband, it all could have been avoided.

When the shock began to wear off, Becky looked at him with wounded green eyes that about broke his heart.

"I... I thought I'd never see you again," she stuttered. "And Sara. God Gus, I was so scared."

He brushed tender fingers over her lips. "Hush, it's

over now. I'm sorry I didn't get here in time to stop him before he..."

She clasped his hand and kissed the palm. "It doesn't matter. You're here now and we're going to be okay. Aren't we?" Her eyes, as bright as the stars above, filled with hope and longing and—love.

Gus's heart surged with happiness and he smiled.

"We're going to be just fine." And he did what he'd been longing to do for what felt like forever, he kissed the woman he vowed to love and cherish for the rest of their lives.

Afterword

Reviews are the lifeblood of any successful author. Without you, we can't be heard.

If you enjoy the story, please consider sharing on your favorite social media sites, as well as GoodReads and from wherever you've bought the book.

Thank you,

Jacquie Biggar

Jacqbiggar.com

About the Author

JACQUIE BIGGAR is a USA Today bestselling author of Romantic Suspense who loves to write about tough, alpha males who know what they want, that is until they're gob-smacked by heroines who are strong, contemporary women willing to show them what they really need is love. She is the author of the popular Wounded Hearts series and has just started a new series in paranormal suspense, Mended Souls.

She has been blessed with a long, happy marriage and enjoys writing romance novels that end with happily-ever-afters.

Jacquie lives in paradise along the west coast of Canada with her family and loves reading, writing, and flower gardening. She swears she can't function without coffee, preferably at the beach with her sweetheart. :)

Sign up now to keep up with Jacquie's new releases, excerpts, giveaways, and more:

Newsletter

jacqbiggar.com
jbiggar@jacqbiggar.com

facebook.com/jacqbiggar

twitter.com/jacqbiggar

instagram.com/jacqbiggar

amazon.com/author/jacquiebiggar

bookbub.com/authors/jacquie-biggar

goodreads.com/JacquieBiggar

Also by Jacquie Biggar

Wounded Hearts Series

Tidal Falls

The Rebel's Redemption

Twilight's Encore

The Sheriff Meets His Match

Summer Lovin'

Wounded Hearts Box Set

Maggie's Revenge

With This Heart

Mended Souls Series

The Guardian

The Beast Within

Gambling Hearts

Hold 'Em

Crazy Little Thing Called Love

Blue Haven

Sweetheart Cove

Single Titles

Silver Bells

The Lady Said No

My Baby Wrote Me A Letter

Tempted by Mr. Wrong

Valentine: A Hearts and Kisses Romance

Preview Hold 'Em- A Gambling Hearts Novel

BY JACQUIE BIGGAR

Matthew Shaughnessy tapped the two crappy cards lying face down on the table and prayed for something better. There were three men left, including him, after what had turned out to be an all-night poker match with some of the best players it had ever been his misfortune to come up against.

The dealer kept eyes down and slid three cards off the top with a flick of mobile fingers. Matt's gaze circled the table, landing for an intimidating moment on each opponent. They stared back, doing their level best to catch the minutest tell—if he gave one away.

He wouldn't.

The pile of chips in the middle had grown to gargantuan heights, enough to tempt even the most hardened gambler to give up his life savings.

Matt had.

He needed this win.

The Arab on his right in flowing white robes, fidgeted. That was a good sign. He had shit cards too, then.

So it was between him and the Canadian diplomat. Interesting. The man looked confident, but his pile of chips was dangerously low. This was Matt's chance.

He pushed everything he had left into the pot. "All in," he growled, defying them to match his bet.

The Arab laughed. He shoved his cards and sat back in the velvet upholstered captain's chair. "You play well, my friend. This night is yours. I'm out."

Matt held in his relief, merely nodding and waiting for the Canadian to make his move. The crooning voice of Michael Bublé drifted into the private chambers. Matt glanced up, surprised. He'd been so involved with the game he'd almost forgotten they were in a high-roller room at the casino. He returned his attention to Gardener, willing him to give up, throw in the towel so they could all go home.

Perspiration dotted the man's brow. He used the napkin under his watered down scotch to blot it away with the air of a dying man headed for the gallows. The dealer glanced at Matt with a you-got-this gleam in his eye.

Gardener lifted his cards one-by-one, and the expression of glee that passed over his face made Matt's stomach drop through the floor. The vision he had of a beach vacation with a hot babe faded. Instead, he was now going to have to figure out how he was going to keep the promise he'd made to help his family out of their financial disaster. They were counting on him to save the ranch that had been in their family for over one hundred years.

And he'd just gambled it all away.

Dammit, he'd known he was taking a chance. Disgusted, he slugged back the whiskey, breathing through the fire as it burned its way into his roiling gut, and grabbed his cowboy hat on the back of his chair, preparing to leave the room with his tail between his legs.

"You no play hand?" the Saudi asked, disappointment at losing his night's entertainment clear in his expression.

"I... I can't." The desperation in the Canadian's tone arrested Matt's departure. He eased back into his seat, hope rising faster than a Texas tornado.

The man rolled his chips into the middle, but he was way short of the wagered amount. "Will you accept an IOU?" he begged, biting his lip and guarding those damn cards.

Matt hesitated, loathe to win this way, but

unwilling to give it away either. "House rules, man. No cash, you forfeit the game."

Gardener eyed the pile of chips like a starving man catching a whiff of a sixteen-ounce steak. Suddenly, he turned and dug into his jacket pocket. Matt stiffened. Was he going to pull a flipping gun on them?

Instead of a derringer, the man held out a diamond ring, nestled in the palm of his hand. "Will you accept this as a token?"

Matt sucked in a surprised whistle. The ring was a beaut. A center stone, at least two carats, and surrounded by a ring of blue fire. Sapphires. It had to be fate. How else could he account for the fact that he stood a chance of winning the bounty of a lifetime?

"Where did you get that?" he demanded, his grip turning white where it wrapped around the arm of his chair.

Gardener looked at the ring and shrugged. "It's been in my wife's family for generations. My daughter is getting married next weekend and has always wanted this to be her wedding ring. I brought it to be cleaned but got sidetracked by this game. She's going to hate me if I don't have it to pass on to her husband." He tapped his cards confidently. "Good thing I don't have to worry about that, right gentlemen?"

The Arab crossed his arms and gazed back and forth between them, obviously getting as much enjoyment out of this turn of events as he did the game he'd just lost over a hundred-fifty grand playing.

Matt wavered between doing what he knew was right—his momma had ingrained the life lesson into his head—and grabbing the money and getting while the getting was good.

Aw, shit.

He couldn't do it. Fair was fair.

"Throw it in there," he grumbled, ignoring the Arab's chuckle.

Gardener wheezed out a relieved sigh and dropped the ring on the pile seemingly without a thought to its legacy.

"Call," he quipped, triumphant. He flipped his cards over in a fan proving why he'd been so damn sure of himself—a full house, jacks high.

He rubbed his chubby hands together and reached out to pull the winning pile his way.

A euphoric sense of accomplishment twisted Matt's lips into their first true smile of the night. "You might want to hold up there, partner. You haven't seen my hand yet."

Both men leaned forward. One with interest. The other with a growing look of dread.

Matt displayed his cards one by one.

Queen of hearts. Queen of spades. Two of clubs. Queen of clubs.

Even the crooning Bublé went silent in anticipation.

Queen of diamonds. Four of a kind.

Matt had just become the proud owner of a stranger's diamond ring.